# TWISTED TAPESTRIES

Jenna Pascoe is a Cornish fisherman's daughter. When her parents receive news that her mother's sister, aunt Olive, is coming home to England from Italy, they refuse to acknowledge her. Family secrets resurface and Jenna's initial delight turns to dismay. However, Olive and her family turn up at their home, and Jenna meets her handsome cousin Alessandro. How will the families resolve their differences — and how will cousins, Jenna and Alessandro cope with their growing feelings for each other . . . ?

JOYCE JOHNSON

# TWISTED TAPESTRIES

*Complete and Unabridged*

# LINFORD
*Leicester*

First published in Great Britain in 2007

First Linford Edition
published 2008

Copyright © 2007 by Joyce Johnson

British Library CIP Data

Johnson, Joyce, *1931 –*
    Twisted tapestries.—Large print ed.—
Linford romance library
    1. Cousins—Fiction 2. Family secrets—Fiction
    3. Cornwall (England: County)—Fiction
    4. Love stories 5. Large type books
    I. Title
    823.9'14 [F]

    ISBN 978–1–84782–339–7

Published by
F. A. Thorpe (Publishing)
Anstey, Leicestershire

Set by Words & Graphics Ltd.
Anstey, Leicestershire
Printed and bound in Great Britain by
T. J. International Ltd., Padstow, Cornwall

# 1

Jenna Pascoe tossed the last crusty piece of pasty high in the air. A watchful seagull squawked, neatly caught it and carried it away. 'Best pasty in Cornwall that is. My mother made it so you're a lucky gull.' She tied her thick dark curls away from her face with a piece of frayed rope from the deck of the family fishing boat, *Cornish Star*. 'That's better,' she said to Rob, her younger brother, 'now I can see what sort of catch we've got.'

'Pretty fair,' her father, Sam Pascoe replied. 'Fetch a bob or two in the market and still plenty left for ourselves.' He grinned at his pretty daughter. 'A good supper tonight for us and for the lodgers, plenty mackerel and some grand bass.'

'Best be heading back.' Rob folded up the nets. 'Ma is counting on us getting back with this fish before tea time.'

'It's such a grand day though, it seems too nice to go in.' Jenna sorted the silver fish into wicker baskets.

'Mebbe one more cast,' Sam said.

'No.' Rob jerked his head towards the horizon. 'There's cloud building up, let's not push our luck. It's been a good day.'

'Rightio.' Sam amenably went into the boat's tiny engine shed. 'Though we've plenty of time before visitors have their teas.' The engine coughed, spluttered and died. Sam tried again — cough, splutter, silence.

Rob dropped his net on the deck. 'Here, let me have a go, you've not got the right touch. She needs nursing.'

'Huh, replacing more like. It's so old I can't even remember buying it.'

'You didn't, it was second hand — or fifth hand more like.' Rob pulled the starter. 'There, told you, a light touch . . . ' But the engine died again and the small boat rocked as the smooth surface of the ocean gently rippled.

Sam looked anxiously at the sky. 'Come on, Rob, it looks like a squall and it's coming in fast.'

'Just a tick, I can see why . . . ' Rob bent to rummage in the toolbox on the deck, staggered as a wave slapped the boat. 'Oops.' He straightened, bent back to the engine and after a few uneasy seconds it fired and maintained a steady note.

'What a genius of a brother. Well done, Rob. Head for home, Dad, and don't spare the horses.'

'Will do.' Sam took the wheel. 'Somehow we've got to get a new engine, or a reconditioned one. This one's done for.'

'Let's hope it'll be a good season,' Jenna said, 'but the house is getting shabby. We'll never attract a good tourist trade if the place is falling to bits.'

Jenna was silent. She was struck with a pang of guilt, too, for her lovely day out with her father and brother. She should have stayed at home to help out, but her mother had said she could manage, and at least they'd be bringing home much needed food. But she was anxious now to be back.

'Best tidy up the deck,' Sam called out. 'Batten down what you can and stow the rest in here. Lash the fish baskets secure.' Superstitiously he patted the old engine.

He could usually feel a storm coming but his instincts had deserted him this time. It had been such a grand day out and, although he hated to admit it, it was a relief to be away from the house for a while. But as the first rumble of thunder cracked the air, he had an awful foreboding he may have pushed the Pascoe luck too far once too often. Jagged lightning danced on a dark horizon, large drops of rain splashed on to the deck and a stormy wind whipped up crested waves.

'Get the oilskins,' Sam yelled from the wheelhouse. But Jenna shook her head, too busy trying to secure the baskets of fish. As the boat rocked, they slid about on the slippery deck and she found it hard to hold them.

Rob threw her a thick rope. 'Tie the handle to that bracket. I'll lash this one to the mast and the weight should keep them steady.'

'I can't hold this one,' Jenna cried as the rain hissed down in sheets. Her hands were soon cold and wet, the thick rope difficult to tie.

'Hang on.' Rob lurched towards her, but at that moment the boat plunged down into a huge wave and the panniers of fish went crashing into the side of the tipping vessel. For a terrible second it looked as though the *Cornish Star* was going to capsize into a watery grave. It held at a sharp angle for a split second then, with a juddering heave it righted, but not before the panniers had been thrown overboard and the precious catch returned to the seabed.

'No.' Rob raced across the deck in a

vain attempt to save at least one of the baskets before it disappeared.

'Rob,' Jenna shrieked as he missed his footing on the fish-slippery deck. The boat wallowed down into the trough of the next wave and the prow went under water. She took a deep breath before she went with it, clinging on to the side.

She was near the wheelhouse and Sam, hanging on to the wheel with one hand, grabbed his daughter with the other, dragging her into shelter. 'Don't be scared, Jen, it'll blow over as swift as it came up.'

'I'm not scared. It's Rob, I can't see him.' Her voice was fearful. 'I think he's overboard . . . '

'Take the wheel, hold it steady. I'll go see . . . '

'No, Dad. He's in the sea. He fell.' She was already stripping off her heavy top and trousers, kicking off her sea boots. 'Best you hold the boat steady.'

'No, you can't . . . '

'Course I can.' She managed a damp

grin. 'Anyway, I'm a better swimmer than you.'

'Jenna, come back here at once . . .' But she was already outside, blinded by the stinging rain, fighting the wind but noting the thunder was already marginally less noisy.

'Rob,' she yelled, clinging to the boat's side as she moved up and down its length, peering through the rain. She called again and again but the still-angry sea mocked her with silence. 'Rob, please . . . please.'

He was a strong swimmer but she thought he might have knocked his head as he fell. The only sound was the mournful sound of the foghorn Sam was pulling. The squall was blowing itself out and the sea was calming down.

'Rob,' Jenna kept calling as the sea began to calm and the rain stopped. There was still a steep swell as she leaned over the side and a familiar line of rocks appeared ahead — The Dragon's Teeth, the first dangerous landmark towards the shelter of Polgrehan harbour. Still no sign of Rob, Jenna felt despair and she thought he must have been knocked unconscious, unable to hold his own against the sea.

'Rob,' she sobbed then stopped — there was something on the rocks ahead, a dark shape, a human arm flung out but the body — so still. 'Dad,' she called back, 'there's someone on the rocks. It must be Rob.'

'Is he all right?' Sam shouted.

'I don't know. I'm going to him. Take care, don't come too close to the rocks. I can swim out.' She jumped over the side, too dangerous to dive. There were treacherous submerged rocks guarding the Teeth, but she was a Cornish water baby and knew the ridge better than her own face. It held no terrors for her, her fear was for that still figure on the rocks.

Jenna reached and rocks and yelled back, 'It is Rob, unconscious but still breathing.'

'Thank you, Lord.' Sam lifted his

eyes to the heavens where the clouds had already lightened, streaks of blue painting out the stormy grey.

Jenna slid back into the water, turned her back, manoeuvred Rob in front of her and kicked away from the rocks back to the boat, clasping Rob's head between her hands. Holding him upright, she trod water as Sam leaned down and hauled his son aboard. She heaved herself over the side, back in the safety of the Cornish Star.

Sam put his head to Rob's chest. 'Heartbeat's strong. Turn him over, his lungs'll be waterlogged.'

'He was on his stomach, he'd been sick, his head's bleeding.'

Rob stirred, moaned, shivered and retched up water. 'What happened? My head's thumping.'

'Thank God it's no worse,' Sam said. 'You tumbled over the side, washed up on the Teeth. Jen swam to fetch you back.'

'Thanks, Jen . . . but the catch? I tried to save it. Oh, Lord.'

'All gone back where it came from, but don't you worry, we'll get you to the doctor's.'

'I'm all right, I don't need a doctor. But Mum, she'll be mad. That fish was for the visitors' tea. She'll be some cross.'

'Not when I tell her what happened, I'll see to that.' Sam spoke with a bravado he didn't feel and Jenna's spirits, buoyed by Rob's rescue, took a sudden downturn followed by a pang of guilt for leaving her mother to cope with her busy day on her own.

As they reached the back door, they heard a querulous wail. Sam frowned. 'Clarrie off again, a bad sign.' He pushed open the back door. 'Here we are Mary, love, back to bother you.' His voice was overly bright.

'You've taken your time.' Mary Pascoe banged her flat iron on to a white bed sheet and looked at her family with aggrieved hostility. 'I thought you were never coming back. Clarrie is so fretful, I've hardly had a minute and visitors'll be in for tea soon and I haven't had a second to lay up tables. Here,' she rested the iron on its stand, picked up the crying infant from the floor and thrust her towards Jenna, 'you try with her, she's been at it all day. I could have done with some help today.'

'But, Mum, you said it would be all right.'

'Well, I'll know better next time . . . ' she broke off. 'Lord above, look at you all, drowned rats, dripping all over.'

'Mary.' Sam put a placatory hand on his wife's arm, wondering not for the first time, where the sweet, laughing girl he'd married twenty years ago had disappeared to.

He knew she had to work hard to make ends meet and the unexpected appearance of Clarrie, lovely child though she was, had added to Mary's burden of toil.

He cleared his throat. 'Now, Mary, don't be cross. The weather blew up, you must have heard the storm. Rob here had a terrible accident, fell overboard and hit his head. He might have died if Jenna hadn't jumped in the sea and swan to Dragon's Teeth to get him off the rocks.'

Mary's face paled as she put her hand to her heart. 'Nearly died!' She took a breath and reached out to touch her son's shoulder. 'Rob, are you all right? Truly? There's blood in your hair and you're soaking wet.'

She reached out to Jenna. 'And you're soaked, too,' She took Clarrie out of Jenna's arms. 'That was brave of you to rescue your brother. Thank the Lord no harm came to either of you. Now, upstairs to get dry clothes on. When you're ready and if you're sure you're both fit, I need help with supper. Let's get the fish cleaned and gutted, and Rob, when I've seen to your head, there's a pail of spuds outside to be peeled and cut up for chips. Mr and Mrs Arkwright want supper early. They're taking a bus ride to Truro.'

There was silence. Jenna and Rob looked at Sam.

'Er . . . the accident. I'm 'feared the fish went overboard with Rob. He was trying to save them — good catch it was too. Boat near capsized, but 'twas too late to . . .'

'No fish?' Mary's voice rose. 'I was counting on it for tea. Now what am I to do? There's Mr Tregenna, Miss Phillips and four visitors. Six suppers to find as well as ours.'

'There's lots of eggs, Mum,' Jenna said, 'and I can run to the shops for some ham.'

'Shop's closed by now, you're that late.' Mary's lips tightened.

'I'll knock him up. Joe Varcoe never minds opening up in an emergency. Let me take Clarrie, he loves to see her, always gives her a gingerbread.'

Mary sat down heavily, head in hands. 'All right, no option, I suppose.' She turned to Sam. 'And the insurance man called earlier. Boat insurance has elapsed, well overdue he says and he can only stretch it for a couple of days. Be back Wednesday — and I'm out of housekeeping, so Joe will just have to put it on the slate.'

Fortunately Joe's boys had had a good catch and he was willing to part with enough for six suppers. 'Tell your ma I'll put it on the account. Some storm earlier, hope you weren't out in it. Visitors, is it — the fish? Not sure I should let you have it for they tourists. Permanent lodgers, I don't mind, and Miss Phillips is a teacher up at the school here. She's from Plymouth mind, but she can't help that.' He threw the fish on the scales.

'I like the tourists,' Jenna said, 'they bring us a bit of life, and money into the village, some in your shop, I dare say.'

He wrapped up the fish and made a note in his book. 'Tell your dad I'll mebbe see him in The Pilchards tonight, and say . . . '

'I will. Thanks.' Jenna waved from the doorway. Joe had been widowed three months ago. His sons were grown up and away and he was a lonely man, always eager for a chat.

'Thank the Lord.' Mary Pascoe was mollified by the fish and Rob had finished chipping potatoes, none the worse for his accident, and was cutting up saffron cake.'

Her mother looked so tired and careworn, Jenna put her arm round her. 'Don't be worried. I'm sorry I went out today. I'll make it up to you. We'll manage. More tourists will be here soon for the summer season.'

'You could take that job at the big house, Lady Poultner's looking for a parlour maid.'

'I don't want to be a parlour maid,' Jenna said sharply. 'I'm happy here, helping you and . . . '

'When you're not out fishing or beachcombing or crabbing.'

'That's not fair. I go out mainly in the evenings when the work's done. Today was an exception and you said . . . '

'Your brother, Matthew, loves it at the Hall. He's second in charge at the stables now and you're eighteen years old, time you thought of settling.'

'Settling?'

'Either married with a home of your own or some sort of job. Mr Johns, the hairdresser, is looking for a new apprentice. Oh, and Joshua called today looking for you — you could do worse.'

'Mother!' Jenna's dark blue eyes flashed. 'I have no talent of hairdressing, I can't even cope with my own hair. Do you want to get rid of me? I'm, not walking out with Joshua either, he's a friend from schooldays.'

Mary's hands were still, then she placed the neat fillets of white fish on an enamel plate. 'Joshua seems to think you're more than that. Reach me the flour, love. No, I don't want to be rid of you, but it's no life for you here. Look at Miss Phillips now, earning good money, saving for her bottom drawer for when she marries that chap from Plymouth. Well respected she is.'

'I don't want to be teacher either, and she'll have to give it up anyway when she's married. That's the law these days.'

'Anyway, are the tables laid and has Rob finished the chips?' Mary chose to ignore Jenna's last remark.

'Yes they are, and yes he has, and there are the Arkwrights. I'll make the tea.' Jenna put on a clean apron and took a plate of bread and butter into the dining room.

It was nearly two hours before the family sat down to their own supper in the kitchen of Harbour View, a substantial stone house left to Mary Pascoe on her parents' death. Sam Pascoe had once had a good job at the local shipwrights, but that closed down and he had been out of work for many months before he and Mary had hit on the idea of running Harbour View as a boarding house for permanent lodgers or passing tourists.

Mary was a good cook and a good manager, but the summer season was short, times were hard and the house was showing its age, much in need of costly refurbishment for which Sam and Mary just didn't have the money.

The family supper was a much more modest affair than that of their visitors. 'That fish looked grand,' Sam said, regretfully cutting himself a hunk of bread and cheese.

'They all enjoyed it.' Jenna poured tea and got a bottle of beer for her father.

'Lucky for some,' Rob said.

'I'm too tired to eat a thing,' Mary said. 'I'll just have some tea.'

'Mr Tregenna looked some smart tonight,' Jenna smilingly said, 'new suit, flower in button-hole . . . '

'Got a fancy woman.' Sam yawned.

'Don't be disgusting.' Mary was acid. 'Mr Tregenna's a gentleman, the perfect lodger.'

'Well, he's been a widower for ten years, give him a chance,' Sam replied.

Mary shut her eyes with an exasperated sigh. The family ate in silence for some minutes then Mary opened her eyes, slapped her hand down on the tabletop and looked sternly at her husband and children. 'There have to be some changes,' she said, I can't put up with this any longer. I'm so tired every day, up and down stairs, cleaning, cooking, seeing to Clarrie.'

'Jenna helps, don't you?' Sam frowned at his daughter.

'I do try. Today . . . '

'I don't want to hear anything more about today, it's all the tomorrows I'm thinking about.' Mary looked directly at her husband. 'You could be more help here. You promised when we started this business. 'Anything, I'll do anything my dear', you said. Where's all that now? You're off most of the time in that leaky old boat, hardly catch enough fish to pay for its keep, or you're at The Three Pilchards. Well, I've had enough of it.'

Sam lit his pipe and eyed the door. 'You're overtired, Mary, it's been a bad day all round. I will help more and I'll see Bert Grundya about some chickens. I think you're hard on Jenna, she does her share.'

'She needs to get a job. Most days she finds time to go to the beach swimming and you encourage her to go fishing with you. It's time for changes,' she poured herself more tea, 'and we're in debt to half the tradesmen in the village.' She sat up straight and spoke briskly, 'We need more cash coming in. Rob, there's a job for you at Poulter's. Matthew's spoken up for you as an under gardener.'

'But I don't know a thing about gardening, fishing's my job — with Dad.'

'You'll soon learn and your sort of fishing isn't bringing enough money in. Jenna, you could start as a parlour maid, it's four days a week including weekends if there's a house party. Wages aren't bad, you've food and keep so you'll have some money to bring home.'

A thin cry from upstairs broke the

silence that followed, 'I'll see to her,' Jenna said.

'No, I will. You all just think what I've said.'

The stillness lasted until Sam knocked out the ashes of his pipe, put it in his pocket and took his coat from behind the door. 'Anyone want me, I'm at The Pilchards.'

# 2

Hundreds of miles away from Polgrehan, across the European continent the small Italian town of Santini had a precarious foothold near the base of the Abruzzi mountains. Santini was really hardly more than a small village, but its inhabitants were proud of its fine old church and lively market square. The Trattoria di Mascio was the only eating place in the square and indeed in the town itself.

One hot early spring day Olivia di Mascio was preparing pasta for the lunchtime trade. Her young son, Carlo, was setting out tables on the rough stone terrace outside the restaurant. It was a spring day such as the one in which the Pascoes in Cornwall had started out on their ill-fated fishing trip, but in Santini, instead of a sudden tempestuous squall, the air was curiously sultry, not a breeze stirred the trees and the usual chatter of song birds was muted. It seemed the very atmosphere held its breath.

Olivia, a handsome dark-haired woman well into middle age, came out on to the terrace, her hands white with flour. She briefly scanned the sky, 'Carlo, bring the tables back towards the trellis, the sun's hot, it will be better to eat in the shade of the vines.'

Carlo, a strong boy of fourteen, nodded as he set out carafes of rough red wine made by the di Mascios from their small vineyard on the lower slopes of Santini mountain.

Back in the cool darkness of the kitchen Olivia pounded yellow dough until it became smooth and elastic enough to pass through her ancient pasta machine. A little girl sat in a high chair nearby playing with some dough, moulding shapes and dropping them on the floor with a little shriek of delight.

'No, no, Francesca, you mustn't do that. Make a small ball, see, like Granny.' The child simply laughed and flung the dough across the room. Olivia wagged her finger and shook her head at the child then divided her own dough into six pieces and covered all but one with a cloth.

She found it impossible to chide the toddler — the tragedy of whose mother's death still weighed so heavily on her. Marietta di Mascio, Olivia's only daughter, had been dead for over a year, but the ache in Olivia's heart never lessened. The child, Francesca, was so like her mother it was almost too much to bear, but she had to bear it to make a life for Francesca, Marietta's sad legacy to her family. Olivia cradled the baby close, kissed her, then set her down gently, 'Shoo, go to Uncle Carlo.'

Francesca tottered off happily and Olivia turned back to her stove where a rich aromatic tomato sauce simmered. She added herbs, stirred, tasted and put the spoon down with a satisfied smile. Perfect.

An hour later the trattoria was almost full, the mid-day meal in full swing, plates of the home-made pasta and home-grown salads covering the tables. Olivia's pasta was famous and business men from the nearby larger town came to eat lunch at di Mascio's.

Vittoria, a dark-haired very pretty girl from the village was an added attraction — she swished flirtatiously between the tight-packed tables, clearing dishes, replenishing wine and chatting to the mainly male customers.

When the last customer had been served Olivia came out of the kitchen to talk to her regulars. All greeted her courteously, several stood and kissed her on both cheeks as they complimented her on her food.

'Wonderful.'

'Delicious. Amazing how you keep up the standard.'

'The ice cream, better than ever — fit for the best restaurants in Italy.'

Olivia laughed off the compliments. 'I'm happy enough in Santini,' she replied, 'this is where I was so happy with Angelo, my husband. It was his mother, Annunziata, who taught me how to cook and I owe it to her and Angelo to carry on the di Mascio tradition.

'You should re-marry,' the bolder windowers would say, 'a widow for four years — too long for such a fine-looking woman,' and the accompanying wink meant, 'and here I am, available and willing.'

'Such nonsense,' Olivia would reprimand the speaker with a sharp thump on the shoulder as she presented him the bill.

One or two diners still lingered over a final glass of wine inside the trattoria. Olivia served them coffee, then carried the family tray outside to a small table in an open-sided shed which protected the entrance to the wine cellar where the di Mascio wines were stored in casks.

'So busy today,' Vittoria spooned up the rapidly-melting ice-cream greedily. She waved to the last diners who were leaving the trattoria.

'See you tomorrow, Signor Crolla,' Olivia called out.

'Hope so,' he replied but his companion pointed to the sky with a grimace.

'See the clouds round the top of Santini Mountain? That's ash, and more than usual. One day . . . '

'Mount Santini will erupt,' Carlo laughed. 'You've been saying that for as long as I can remember.'

'You'll see. One day,' the man repeated, having the last word as usual before the two men left.

Vittoria put down her cup, 'I must go too, my auntie's coming later. I need to help with the baking. How's Alessandro?' she said casually to Olivia.

'Doing fine,' Olivia's face lit up, 'his uncle has made him manager and he's going to build a fine new ice-cream parlour in Florence. He's got a lovely flat overlooking the water. We're going to spend the winter there and Carlo will see how a business is run.'

'You're not leaving here?' Vittoria looked alarmed.

'No, no, just a winter break. I don't suppose I shall ever leave Santini.'

'Will Alessandro ever come back?'

'Not to live.' Olivia put her hand on the girl's arm, 'I'm sorry, I know you like my son a good deal, but he is so ambitious and there's nothing for him here. He is a good son, he sends money home, I doubt I could keep the trattoria on without his help.'

She shrugged her shoulders expressively, she didn't want to give lovesick Vittoria hope for the future. The two had been good childhood friends but that was all. He would never return permanently to Santini.

Impulsively Vittoria bent to kiss her employer — she was very fond of all the di Mascios.

But it was several days before they saw Vittoria again and by that time the lives of many people in Santini had changed dramatically.

Just before dawn the following day, Mount Santini erupted sending showers of rocks, boulders and lava down towards the village. Miraculously, because of the heat, the di Mascios had moved their mattresses into the open-sided lean-to by the wine cellar. That action probably saved their lives. A huge boulder crashed on to the trattoria, the roof caved in but the lean-to remained intact. The noise was terrible and Olivia had been sure they would all be killed.

In the dawn light she, Carlo and Francesca joined the stunned villagers to assess the situation. Many homes had been destroyed, lives lost and injuries suffered. The road out of the village was no more than a track and would certainly be blocked. It could be hours, days even, before medical and relief teams could reach the isolated village. News of the disaster would be slow to spread to the cities where most of the assistance would be mobilised.

The di Mascio trattoria was badly damaged, equipment and stores unusable, only the wine cellar being untouched. Carlo brought up some barrels to share with the villagers and the ruined trattoria became a focal gathering point to pool provisions, share information and bring comfort to the bereaved and injured.

On the second day after the volcano had erupted the villagers gathered outside the trattoria for their midday meal, a communal picnic, where fallen rocks served as seats and tables. The mood was sombre, the losses of relatives, homes and belongings finally beginning to sink in. Although the one doctor in the village had worked day and night several villagers were in dire need of hospital treatment and anxiety was written on many faces.

As people finished their meal and began drifting back to their homes there was a great shout and a young man came running towards them, waving his arms. 'A truck,' he yelled, 'a truck's coming down the valley — and a Red Cross van. Thank God, help's coming.'

They all watched as the vehicles drew closer. Progress was slow, huge rocks were strewn across the track and at one point men got out of the vans and manhandled the rocks away.

Olivia craned her neck to see and caught her breath as a tall dark-haired man jumped back into the lead vehicle. 'Carlo,' Olivia clutched her son's arm, 'can you see from here, your eyes are younger than mine — the man driving the first vehicle — could it be . . . ?'

The driver of that first rescue van was her dearest eldest son, Alessandro. He would know what she should do next. Angelo's death, then Marietta's, she'd struggled to do the right thing but now, Nature's last blow had knocked the fight out of her. Alessandro would help her.

As the vans drove into the village square the villagers flocked to welcome them. Olivia was one of the first and as the men climbed wearily out she ran to her son and embraced him, 'Alessandro, thank God you've come. It's wonderful to see you.'

'You're safe, Mamma. Carlo? Francesca?'

'Right behind me.'

Carlo hugged his brother, Francesca plucked at his legs. 'Me, me.' She lifted up her arms and Alessandro laughed as he picked her up.

In the market square Alessandro was made much of. Everyone knew of his business success in Florence and Rome and they were proud of the local boy made good. If a son of Angelo di Mascio could make it maybe their own sons could find wealth in the cities instead of enduring the grinding poverty of rural Santini.

Olivia watched keenly as he listened to everyone, nodded, and promised help was coming from the cities. She sighed remembering how deeply she'd fallen in love with Angelo, his thick dark hair and brown eyes — very strangely similar to Alessandro's. She'd always believed it was God's reward to preserve their secret.

It seemed an age to Olivia before the market square was deserted and she and Carlo and Alessandro were alone on the trattoria's terrace. She put Francesca down for a nap then poured out glasses of deep red wine. 'At least the wine was saved. Your father was so proud of his vineyard.'

Alessandro raised his glass, 'To Father,' he said quietly. 'He loved Santini and the rural life here, he was never interested in the ice-cream business.'

'No . . . he was a disappointment to his grandfather and . . . ' she broke off abruptly and took a sip of wine.

'To Father,' echoed Carlo. He too was delighted to see his older brother. Carlo was a good son, a hard worker, but the responsibility of looking after his mother and little niece weighed heavily on his young shoulders.

'So, we have to assess the damage

and see what you want to do, Mamma.'

'It can be repaired I suppose, we've been luckier than some, but somehow for me the heart has gone since Angelo, then Marietta . . . now this. Carlo has been a stalwart. I couldn't have managed without him or without your financial help, Alessandro, but now . . . ' She spread her hands, 'I'm not getting any younger.'

'I can take care of the reconstruction, spend some time here, but do you want to stay in Santini?'

Olivia looked startled, 'Where else would we go? This is our home.'

'Let's go inside and see.' Alessandro stood up and gave his mother his arm. 'Carlo, you too must say how you like to see your future.' He picked up a sleepy Francesca. 'And you, little one — but you will have to trust us to decide for you.'

Some hours later the di Mascios ate a cold supper by flickering candlelight. Alessandro's van had been packed with food supplies which had already been distributed to the villagers in desperate need.

'Other help is on the way, the newspapers and radio are launching appeals. Santini has a future, it can all be put together again if that's what you want, Mamma.'

'What choice do I have? It will be costly to restore the trattoria, hard work, no money . . . '

'You know you never have to worry about that, I and the uncles will take care of it all — if it IS what you want. For a start you could come and live in Florence, my apartment is large, Carlo could join the business, you could be a lady of leisure and Francesca could grow up as a Florentine lady.

'Florence! I've never been . . . '

'Mamma,' he interrupted gently, 'you have never been anywhere but Santini since you were a very young girl. You need a rest, see more of Italy, travel . . . '

'I'm not sure I'd like the city life for ever. Perhaps a visit.'

'That can easily be arranged, but there is another alternative.'

'And what's that?'

There was a long pause while Alessandro poured more wine from a large earthenware jug, miraculously intact. 'You could return to your own country, visit your own family.'

He concentrated on the wine, not choosing to meet his mother's eyes.

There was a long silence before Olivia stood up and began clearing the dirty plates. She was agitated, clattering dishes together at random, her breath short and rasping.

'Sit down, Mamma.' Alessandro gently took the plates from her and led her back to sit down. 'Drink,' he put the flask into her hands. Even in the candlelight he could see how white her tanned face was.

'No, no, I couldn't go back, you don't know . . . '

'I do, of course I do. It would be painful, but it's over thirty years since you left.'

'And no word,' Olivia burst out bitterly, 'not a single word. I wrote and wrote but they returned my letters. I sent them pictures of you and Carlo. Nothing until fifteen years ago, a short note from a solicitor telling me my parents were dead, but that I had no claim on the estate. I was still disowned, I didn't exist. How could I possibly go back there?'

'You . . . we have family there, aunts, uncles, cousins maybe. Carlos and me, we are half-English. Perhaps this is the time to build bridges, forget the past. Aren't you curious, Mamma, don't you ever think of your early years?'

'I haven't done for a long time, deliberately not. I was hurt, punished, abandoned when I most needed help,' she avoided his direct gaze, 'and in the early days here it wasn't so easy sometimes . . . ' she tailed off, her eyes veiled.

Alessandro sighed, 'Well then, we should be very happy to welcome you all to Florence. It is a beautiful city.'

'Let me think. There's so much has happened here — the shock. I need time. I did . . . do still have a young sister, I hope she knew little of what went on. They kept her away from me — how would I get in touch?'

'Write to your old address would be the first step. I can make enquiries.' Somewhere in the South West of England wasn't it? The very tip, you once showed me on the map, sticking out into the ocean.'

'Cornwall it's called.' Olivia forced her mind back down the years.

'That's the only time you've ever spoken about your past.'

'What would I do there? I should feel like a foreigner, and . . . ' she hesitated again, 'I wasn't popular when I left . . . my marriage to Angelo . . . ?'

Alessandro laughed. 'Here you are Italian, you speak the language, you act like an Italian. In England . . . Cornwall, you would speak English and behave like a Cornishwoman. You are infinitely adaptable, Mamma, that is one of the many things I admire you for'

'I don't want to go to England.' Carlo was dismayed, 'It's cold there and rains all the time.'

'No it doesn't,' his mother protested, 'I can remember beautiful sunny days, we swam in the sea, had picnics, fished from the rocks and . . . '

'You see,' Alessandro said, 'you are back there already. Francesca would love it too. You don't have to stay there for ever, there's always a home for you here.'

'But Carlo . . . ?' Olivia frowned, 'I can see why he wouldn't want to go, he's happy at school here — and he doesn't speak much English.'

'Easy,' Alessandro smiled, 'you know we have some connections in England through our business. There are many Italian families who have left this country to find work and a better life. We have distant cousins in Scotland, the Pablo family have a very successful ice-cream parlour and delivery service in the north of England. I've been thinking for some time of Britain as a new market. Cornwall is a tourist area.

'I shall take you, Mamma, and Francesca to Cornwall to meet our relations and maybe set you up in business there.'

'And me?' Carlo was plaintive, 'I can't stay here on my own.'

'Of course you can't. You shall go to Florence to join your brother, Roberto, who will teach you the business and our uncles will look after you.'

'Florence — I should like that.' Carlo brightened up immediately.

'Mamma?' Alessandro asked.

'I . . . I'm not sure. Let me sleep on it.'

'Of course. Think of it as a holiday, a break, a pause to rest and think. It will take a time to rebuild Santini, I can arrange for the trattoria to be restored. You could let it out or return to run it yourself again if you don't like Cornwall. It will be an escape route if you wish from cold and rainy Cornwall.'

That night, sleeping under the stars, Olivia dreamed of her childhood home in Polgrehan. She'd tried to erase it from her mind. But her dream was a happy one, sea, sun, rocks and sand and a small child running towards her, bucket and spade swinging from her hand. 'Mary!' Olivia said out loud as she woke from her dream.

# 3

It was a calm bright day in Polgrehan some days after Mount Santini's eruption. Few folk there knew of the Italian disaster and it would have meant very little to them. Wireless was still in its infancy and the local press was more concerned with local politics and events.

At Harbour View there was little time for wireless or newspapers. Mary and Jenna had been up since six cleaning, polishing and preparing guests' breakfasts.

Under the new regime Sam was in charge of Clarrie until breakfast was over, Rob, with Jenna, was to serve the guests, clear away, wash up and tidy the kitchen, and on this particular morning Rob was then to go to the big house for an interview with the head gardener.

'I'm not going,' he hissed to Jenna as

they passed each other during the breakfast campaign.

'I don't think there's a choice,' Jenna whispered as she placed a groaning plate before Mr Tregenna.

His eyes lit up, 'Wonderful as usual, I shall miss . . . '

'Something wrong?' Jenna asked.

'Oh no, not at all . . . well yes . . . er . . . I must speak to your mother after breakfast . . . if she's free that is.'

During the post breakfast lull and after Rob had been steered firmly in the direction of Lord and Lady Poultner's, Mr Tregenna knocked tentatively on the kitchen door. In the kitchen Mary tore off her pinafore, wiped her hands, smoothed her hair and opened the door. 'Mr Tregenna — Jenna said you wanted to see me.'

'I do. Just a word.'

Mary closed the door firmly behind her. 'In the parlour please.'

'No, really. I . . . er . . . just . . . '

But Mary was already ushering him into the rarely used front parlour. It smelt of lavender polish, every surface gleamed, but the furniture was shabby and there was a forlorn unloved look about it.

He shuffled his feet nervously.

'I hope everything's all right,' Mary encouraged.

'I shan't be needing the room any longer. I'm . . . um . . . '

Mary flushed, 'Nothing's wrong I hope.'

'No, not at all. I've been very comfortable and happy with you but . . . ' he ended with a rush, 'I'm getting married next month — a lady in Truro, Mrs Fenwick, a widow, a lovely person. We hope you and Mr Pascoe will attend our little ceremony, you've looked after me so well these last five years.'

'Married? Gracious. Oh dear, we'll be sorry to lose you.'

'It's lonely you see, my sons are in Australia, Mrs Fenwick has two daughters and three grandchildren. We all get on well together, it makes me feel quite young again to be with them. Mrs Fenwick and I have bought a small house near the river, I can fish there . . . '

'It sounds grand. Mrs Fenwick is a lucky woman.' Indeed, once the embarrassment of giving notice was done with the old gentleman exuded such an air of contented happiness Mary tried not to be jealous.

'She's a wonderful woman.' He took out his wallet, 'I should like to leave in a day or two.'

'So soon?' Mary was dismayed, a month's rent gone.

'In lieu of notice I shall be pleased to pay two months rent.'

'I couldn't possibly . . . '

'Please,' he pressed notes into her hand.

'Well thank you,' she felt a lump rising as she stood up, 'I must get on.'

'What's up?' Jenna was making a large pot of soup for the lodgers' supper.

'Mr Tregenna's given notice. Getting married.'

'Wow! That's lovely, he's so sweet.'

'Where will we find his like?'

'Plenty more fish in . . . '

'It's not easy. The house is so shabby, Mr Tregenna's been here so long he probably hadn't noticed but that Nottingham couple, they had the cheek to say my sheets were threadbare.'

'Cheer up. I'll make some fresh tea and if you really think it would help if I went up to the Hall I'll give it a try.'

'Oh Jenna,' Mary was close to tears, 'I don't know, I hardly slept last night for worry — but I want to see you get on . . . '

'Not a lot of future as a parlour maid, but if it'll please you . . . '

'Oh, I don't know. I've not been out of the village for three years, and its such hard work, I'm all of a muddle,' she began to sob just as Sam came in with a tub of newly dug potatoes.

He dropped them in alarm when he saw Mary, sending the potatoes rolling all over the floor.

'Now look,' wailed Mary.

'What on earth . . . ?' but Clarrie,

seeing her mother in tears began to wail in sympathy.

'What's to do?' Sam asked as Jenna stooped to gather up the potatoes.

'Mr Tregenna's getting married so Mum's upset — and I'm going to the Hall.'

'But, but . . . ' he put an arm round his wife, 'stop it now, you've set Clarrie off and she can cry for Cornwall if she's a mind to.' He gave Mary his handkerchief, 'I met the postman by the gate.' He put some letters on the table.

'More bills I suppose.' Mary sipped her tea and mopped her eyes.

'Could be some responses to that advertisement I put in a London paper. We're getting more tourists now and it pays to advertise they say,' as he spoke he flipped through the letters, 'here's a strange one, foreign, Italia. We don't know anyone in Italy.' Then he drew in a sharp breath, his face was grave and he passed the envelope to his wife. 'For you, addressed Mary Kittow.'

'Your maiden name, Mum,' Jenna said.

Her mother sat as one in shock, 'It can't be, can it Sam, but these last days I've been unsettled, had a feeling . . . something strange?'

'Open the letter,' Sam said.

'I don't want to. You take it, tear it up — it's too late now.'

Jenna looked puzzled. 'What's the problem? Why won't you open it? Dad, do you know what's wrong?'

'I do, but it's your mother's choice. Let me open it, Mary love. It could be from someone else, someone who's stayed here in the past. We've had a few foreign visitors.'

'No Italians. I'd have remembered that for sure,' she said bitterly.

'Shall I see?'

Sam's thumb was under the envelope flap but Mary sprang up, wrenched it from him, 'No, I know it's her — but I don't want to know, she brought shame on our family, it killed our parents. She doesn't exist as far as I'm concerned.' She flung the envelope into the fire grate, but after the breakfast cooking the range fire was always damped down and the letter rested on the smouldering black slack.

Sam snatched it back, Mary tried to seize it from him but he held her off, 'Where's your Christian charity, woman, your own sister is trying to contact you. For pity's sake see what she has to say . . . '

'Your sister?' Jenna cried out, 'you told us you were an only child. WHERE is your sister? What happened?'

Mary ignored her and sat down pulling the still whimpering Clarrie on to her lap. 'Very well, read it, but Jenna and Clarrie must leave the room.'

'No,' Sam said firmly, 'Jenna's an adult now and she should know the family history. I'm surprised she hasn't heard it in the village before now.'

'Folk are too scared, frightened my father's spirit would haunt them. He decreed SHE was a person with satanic origins.'

'What?' Jenna gasped in astonishment.

'Now, Mary, you know that's nonsense,' Sam rebuked, 'Olive wasn't an evil woman at all.' He didn't add, 'just unfortunate, like thousands of girls before and after her.'

'Olive,' Jenna said, 'I have an Aunt Olive?'

'No, you don't,' Mary said furiously, turning on Jenna as if to strike her.

'Stop it, Mary,' Sam snapped. He opened the letter and extracted the single sheet. After a minute he held out the letter to Mary.

'Tell us, Dad,' Jenny pleaded.

'The letter's from her son, Alessandro di Mascio. He lives in Florence, the address on the letter is Santini. He wants to bring his mother to Cornwall, to Polgrehan.'

'Come here! What for?' Mary said quickly.

'Her village — a volcano erupted destroying their . . . ' he looked at the letter again, 'trattoria.'

'What's that?' Jenna was wide-eyed.

'I think it's a café or restaurant. Olive

has a little girl and two other boys besides Alessandro. The little girl, Francesca, she's coming too.'

'No she isn't, none of them is.' Mary stood up. 'After all these years without a word, not a single word, and now she's down-and-out she wants to creep back here. No, you must write immediately, Sam, and tell this Alessandro that as far as I'm concerned his mother is dead.'

'Mum, that's shocking!'

'Mary.'

'How could you?' Sam and Jenna spoke simultaneously.

'Just do it please,' Mary said to her husband, 'I can't bear to answer her. I'm going to the market, we have a business to run here. I'll take Clarrie, Jenna, you see to the rooms and there are pies to make for supper, along with the soup.'

'But . . . ' Sam held out the letter.

'No!' Mary took her market basket and banged the door behind her.

'What's it all about, Dad? This Olivia

51

di Mascio is my aunt?'

'She is.'

'How?'

Sam took his pipe and sat down. 'I'd better tell you, if you start ferreting around there are a lot of old Polgrehan folk'd tell you any old rubbish. At least I'll tell you the truth.' He filled his pipe while Jenna fretted with impatience. 'Olive Kittow is your ma's older sister and she was engaged to Bert Trelawney, a fisherman from the village. Seemed happy enough until 1902 I think it was — in Feast Week a band of Italian strolling players came to perform in the village hall.

'Angelo de Mascio was one of them, dark, handsome, he had all the maids swooning — but he only had eyes for Olive and she fell for him badly, forgot all about poor old Bert. Wedding was already planned too but Olive was simply head-over-heels in love with Angelo.'

'Goodness, how romantic,' Jenna gasped.

Sam pulled a face, 'Caused an uproar because your granny found out Olive was in the family way. Bert threatened to kill Angelo and your aunt was turned out.'

'How dreadful. How could they be so cruel?'

'I believe they gave her an option of going away, having the baby and putting it up for adoption, but Olive refused, ran away to London and married Angelo. I think they tried to effect a reconciliation with the Kittows before they left for Italy but they point-blank refused and declared their eldest daughter no longer existed — dead in their eyes. Strict Methodists you see.'

'I don't think that's very Christian at all.'

'Well, that's how it was in those days, still is in some cases. Your mother was about ten years old I think. Olive's name was never spoken again except to say she was a wicked girl who'd go to hell and deserved her fate.'

'That's awful, Dad. You can't turn her away. Please, don't write the letter.'

'If I don't your ma will and we've enough worries without shouldering other folks' problems.'

'But she's family, with a little girl the same age as Clarrie.

But in spite of Jenna's protests the letter was written and posted. This was a new side to her mother, all pleas fell on stony ground and eventually Jenna had to give up. And that was the end of it.

Life went on as normal at Harbour View — on the surface, but there was underlying tension. Mary couldn't sleep, Clarrie was fretful, Sam morose, Rob rebellious. He did finally decide to take the gardening post at the Hall but refused to live in.

'No need,' he said firmly, 'I can bike to and fro and still go fishing. You'll see, I'll be a full-time fisherman yet once I've saved enough for my own boat.'

Jenna missed him and their fishing trips together. Sam's boat was in dock and the family budget was tight, Mr Tregenna's regular monthly payment was sorely missed.

Sam had redecorated the room and placed an advert in the local paper and although he still spent many hours in The Pilchards he'd bought some chickens, built a run and was teaching Clarrie how to collect the eggs and help him feed the birds. Nevertheless easy-going Sam was worried, bills were piling up, summer visitors slow to materialise in the damp early season. There was a way he could bring in more money, he'd done it before, but he hated doing it. Mary would kill him if she knew so he was putting it off for as long as possible.

One evening after another damp day, late sunshine enticed the family into the garden. Mary, for once, quietly doing nothing, dozed. Jenna was playing ball with Clarrie who was on a bedtime extension because of lengthening day-light. Sam hoed his greens. It all looked a picture of peaceful harmony until

Jenna stopped in mid-catch, head cocked to one side.

'There's a motor car stopped outside our gate. We don't see many of those in Polgrehan.'

'Mebbe someone about the room,' Sam said eagerly, 'I'll go see.'

Jenna heard the motor drive away, but it was some minutes before Sam came back, perhaps, she thought, he'd been showing someone the room. 'Who was it?' she asked.

Sam opened his mouth in a soundless gasp and looked at Mary who was still asleep. 'They've arrived. I can't send them away.'

'Who, new lodgers?' Jenna threw the ball high and Clarrie laughingly raced to catch it.

'From Italy. Olive Kittow that was and . . .'

'The relatives. Aunt Olive,' Jenna interrupted excitedly.

'And Alessandro and the little one. She's fast asleep, such a long journey for the poor little thing. I've put them

56

in the parlour.' He gently shook his wife's shoulder.

'What?' she started, blinking.

'It's . . . it's Olive, your sister and her son and little girl.'

Wide awake Mary stumbled to her feet. 'Here? But you wrote. Send them away, I can't have her here . . . '

A tall dark man carrying a small child stepped out into the back garden. He approached confidently smiling and Jenna felt a jolt as his dark eyes smiled first at her, then at her mother. 'I couldn't wait, this is a lovely garden and you must be Mary — my aunt.'

He spoke perfect English, just a trace of accent, 'My mother, Olivia de Mascio, is here to see you.' He took Olivia's arm. 'Mamma, speak to your sister please.'

She walked slowly forward. 'Mary?' She was nervous.

Mary blinked. Sam urged her forward, 'They've travelled so far, be charitable, it's your Christian duty. This was your sister's home.'

'It's not hers, it's mine, and they can't stay here.'

'Mother, how can you . . . please, you must speak to them.'

Olivia stood uncertainly, looking from her son to her sister. Alessandro frowned, Francesca woke with a yawn and gave the assembled company a sunny smile, holding her arms out to Mary who flinched and pressed her hand to her heart.

'Of course you must stay here,' Sam said, 'I'm sorry we're unprepared. I did write to you and . . . '

'We had no letter,' Alessandro said, 'since the disaster the post in Santini has been chaotic and I was away from Florence — but I can see we are not welcome. We will leave, find a hotel. Mamma . . . ?'

'No, no, don't,' Jenna said swiftly, 'we have Mr Tregenna's old room, and the attic. There are beds there. I'll get you something to eat and a drink.' She crossed to Olivia, 'I'm Jenna, your niece. I'm happy to see you.'

Olivia smiled and Jenna saw her own mother reflected in Olivia's older face. 'That's kind. Thank you.'

'No, you're our family. Please Mother, I implore you, don't reject your own flesh and blood.'

Mary Pascoe stood aloof, eyes fixed coldly on her sister, 'Why now? All these years — no word. I dreamt of you so often when I was little. I . . . I loved you and you left me — without a word.'

'Not true,' Olive burst out, 'I wrote, many times I wrote to this house and all my letters were returned unopened. When I heard from the solicitor our parents died I gave up. I didn't know you would still be living here. We took a chance coming but hoped whoever lived here now would know of you.'

'We can't support you,' Mary was cold, 'we have a struggle to cope ourselves.'

Alessandro's brow darkened. 'Please understand, we are not here looking for charity. I have ample funds for a hotel, we have family business in Rome,

Venice and soon Florence. We are not poor relations. I persuaded my mother to come here to find her own family. The di Mascios welcomed your sister into our family when she married my father. She is one of us — in Italy we are proud of our family and we support them always.'

His dark eyes flashed, his face flushed with anger, he took his mother's arm and hoisted Francesca higher on his shoulder. 'I'm sorry, Mamma, I made a mistake. We are not wanted here.' His eyes softened a little as he looked at Jenna before turning away.

'No. Stop! You mustn't,' Jenna said desperately. 'Stay. I . . . we want to know you all. My mother has not been herself lately.' She took Mary's hand, 'Please, give your sister your hand, ask her to stay. I'll do anything you want — I'll never go fishing again, I'll go up to the Poultners, I'll work even harder. Mother. PLEASE.'

For a few seconds there was neither sound nor movement, then very slowly

Mary put out her hand briefly to touch her sister's. Her voice was flat but she said, 'Stay . . . if you wish.'

Alessandro shook his head but his eyes held Jenna's, 'No, we cannot . . . '

Olivia stopped him, 'Yes,' then more strongly, 'yes we would like to stay for a while. We will pay our way of course.'

'No need for that,' Sam Pascoe said proudly, 'you'll be our guests.' He shook hands, first with Alessandro, and then after a slight hesitation gave Olivia a quick peck on the cheek

# 4

Nobody knew quite what to do next. Mary went back to her chair, even the confident Alessandro seemed uncertain. Jenna glanced at her father who was looking worried. Only little Francesca knew what to do, she slid out of her brother's arms, toddled over to Clarrie, picked up the ball and with a chuckle tossed it in the air.

Clarrie, after a startled glance at her mother, ran after it, followed by Francesca and their game of catch continued all round the garden, their laughter ringing in the evening air.

Mary's expression softened but she stayed seated staring blankly at her sister. 'I'll make some tea.'

Jenna sprang into action, 'I'll do it, there's some saffron cake and . . . '

'We had supper at the station, please don't worry,' Olivia said, 'tea would be lovely.'

'Shall we stay out here?' Jenna asked, 'it's turned into a fine evening. Our lodgers won't be in for a while, there's a concert down on the quay later.'

'Perhaps we could go,' Alessandro smiled, 'Mamma has a lovely voice.'

'Gracious, I couldn't go down there.' Olivia was shocked, 'Whatever would people think?'

'Does it matter now?' Sam said.

'Well, I'm happy to stay out here,' Olivia said brightly. 'Can I help you, Jenna?'

'No, you sit down — there's a bench over there near your . . . ' she hesitated over the word, ' . . . sister. You surely must want to talk to each other.' There was a note of anxiety in her voice.

'I'll help you,' Alessandro said, 'and . . . er . . . Uncle Sam — can I call you that? I have some Italian wine in my bag, brought especially from our own vineyard.'

'You own a vineyard?' Sam whistled.

'It's only small,' Olivia smiled, 'but

it's good wine. We serve it in our trattoria, or rather used to.'

'The trattoria — it was destroyed?' Jenna asked.

'Yes, but we shall rebuild it, if that's what Mamma wishes.' He smiled at Olivia and put an arm round her. 'She is a strong woman, she will survive,' he whispered to her, 'now go over to your sister, watch the little ones together.' He turned to Sam, 'Shall I get the wine?'

'I suppose so. We've never drunk wine. I can run to The Pilchards and get some cider. Rob, our son, should be here soon, he's training to be a gardener at the big house.'

'Fine, I'll get the wine. Maybe your cider another time. Jenna,' he said her name in a strangely foreign way with emphasis on the 'a'.

Jenna felt a glow as he smiled at her.

'I'll come and help with the tea. That's very English isn't it? Mamma used to tell me about the tea drinking.'

He followed Jenna into the tidy

kitchen where she raked the fire and set the kettle on the range.

'Crockery in that cupboard,' she opened the wooden doors, 'plates, saffron buns in that tin, cheese in the larder, bread and butter . . . but I can manage, you don't have to help.'

'I'd like to. Before I left our village I helped Mamma in the trattoria. I enjoyed it.'

They held each other's eyes for a moment, then looked away.

'Hello. Jenna, what's this? Company?' Her brother, Rob, bounced into the kitchen carrying a basket full of fruit and vegetables, 'Mr Charles said I could pick what I wanted, he's so pleased with me.'

'Lovely, just what we need. Rob, this is Alessandro, our Auntie Olive's eldest son. You know he wrote . . . '

'But I thought Dad wrote and . . . ' Jenna shook her head to silence him.

'They're here now and will stay a while. I'm making tea, Alessandro has some Italian wine and Dad's probably gone to The Pilchards for cider not to be outdone.'

'Wooh — a party. Hello, Alessandro, pleased to meet you.' They shook hands.

'So, you're to be a gardener?'

'No, just biding my time. I'm going to be a fisherman.'

'Like your father?'

'Well, better than Dad. I think I can make a business of it, make a good living.'

'Not many do that,' Jenna said, cutting up fruit cake. 'Alessandro has a business in Florence.'

'Florence!' Rob was impressed.

'A family business. Ice-cream — we make and sell.'

'Jim Penhallorick makes ice-cream in Polgrehan, goes round with a horse and cart and sells it round the villages.'

'Does he now? I must go and visit him.'

'I don't think he'd thank you for it.'

'Why not?'

Rob shook his head, 'You'll see. Half

of the folk around here wouldn't know whether Italy was in China or India.'

'Rob, that's unkind.' Jenna put cheese and pickle on a tray.

'Not really, just that generally folk round here don't travel much.'

'Nothing wrong with that,' Alessandro took the tray from Jenna and carried it through to the garden.

Sam had fetched a flagon of cider, Alessandro opened the wine and poured a little into each glass. As the sun began to sink westwards he proposed a toast — 'To Cornwall and our Cornish family.'

Cautiously they all took a sip and Sam, more used to alcohol than the others, smacked his lips, 'Good stuff,' he pronounced.

Mary shot him a warning glance, set her glass down and poured a cup of tea. Jenna swallowed her wine, it tasted bitter but she finished it out of politeness and felt its relaxing warmth.

Olivia was given Mr Tregenna's old room overlooking the harbour and once inside Harbour View she was quiet, memories flooding back, childhood ones were good, later years less so and the painful way she'd left her home was unbearable. Mary brought towels up to the room and found her sister in tears.

'Mum and Dad's old room,' she said, 'so angry, my last meeting with them, so bitter, dreadful things were said, but for Angelo I don't know what I should have done.'

Mary stood uncertainly by the door, white towels draped over her arm, 'It's been a shock,' she said hesitantly, 'I can't take it in yet — at least Angelo stood by you.' she took a step forward then stopped, 'Perhaps in the morning we'll mebbe talk.'

Olivia dried her eyes, 'Oh I hope so, Mary, there's so much to talk about.'

In the tiny box room along the corridor Jenna made up a camp bed for Alessandro. 'I hope you'll be comfortable — it's a pretty old bed.'

'I shall sleep like a log. Your Cornish air has already made me sleepy.' He took her hand, 'And thank you, Jenna, for persuading us to stay. Mamma would have been so upset to leave.'

'You must forgive my mother, she's been so overworked lately what with the lodgers, tourists and Clarrie, she's not like her old self and she worries a lot, but I do think . . . um, Aunt Olivia will be good for her — as long as they can sort out the past.'

'I hope so too. It's the present that matters, and the future. What's your future, Jenna?'

She smoothed the coverlet on the narrow bed and sat down, 'Ouch! It's really very hard. My future? Up at Poultner Hall looks like,' she pulled a face, 'parlour maid — I don't want to go there one bit.'

'Don't then. Help me.' He sat down beside her, 'I want to see about starting a business in England — I've done some research. You could show us Cornwall, look at its potential. Tourists come here don't they?'

'In the summer, but . . . ' she clasped

her hands, it sounded exciting. 'Why not — if Mother can manage without me.'

'Mamma will help.' He stood up and pulled Jenna to her feet, put his arms around her and went to kiss her cheek but she turned round unexpectedly and their lips met.

The contact was brief, only for a second did his mouth touch hers but they both felt a sensation of shock before he quickly drew back. He pushed his hands through his dark hair, his eyes were puzzled and they held hers for a moment before he turned away and said quietly, 'Goodnight, Jenna, sleep well.'

Next morning Jenna was surprised to find her mother and aunt not speaking much but working harmoniously preparing the guests' breakfasts.

'Couldn't you sleep, Aunt Olivia?' she asked.

'I slept wonderfully thank you dear. The little ones are still fast asleep, they were up so late.'

Later, when the lodgers and visitors had been fed, Alessandro and Sam sat down to eat with the womenfolk. Rob had already left on his bicycle for an early start to his working day. It was strange to see Alessandro and Olivia at the family table, Jenna couldn't quite get used to it and was pleased when Francesca and Clarrie woke up to provide a livelier note to the meal. Mary said very little and it was Sam who first announced his plan for the day.

'I'm off fishing, there are good shoals of mackerel out there and, don't worry, Mary, I did all the chores before breakfast.'

'Can I come along?' Alessandro said, 'and perhaps Jenna too? She promised to show me round the village and harbour.'

'Only if Mum agrees,' Jenna put in swiftly.

''Tis not convenient today,' Sam broke in, 'I've . . . um . . . other business and I've a mate who . . . '

'That's fine, perhaps another time. Can you spare Jenna today, Aunt Mary? And Mamma, what about you?'

'I'm fine here,' Olivia said firmly, 'I'm not ready for the village yet — I rather dread it. I'm very happy to be here with my sister and I'll do whatever Jenna was going to do.'

'Is there a motor garage somewhere where I could rent a car?' Alessandro said.

'There's Jack, right by the harbour, he may have one but his vehicles still have solid tyres. He's the taxi man as well so you'd need to see him.'

Jenna and Alessandro set off from Harbour View down the steep hill towards the harbour. People greeted Jenna, looking curiously at the tall dark stranger accompanying her. She called in the general store to buy lemonade for the picnic, the shop was full and the chattering died away as she and Alessandro went in.

'Morning, Jenna.' Polly Bennet eyed the stranger, 'Visitor?' she asked. Jenna nodded but made no comment as she bought some fruit and lemonade. 'Staying long?' Polly persisted addressing Alessandro direct.

'Maybe.' He smiled at everyone as he and Jenna left the shop.

The speculative buzz of chatter started immediately.

'Five minutes and everyone in the village will know about you, what time you arrived and what you are doing here. The bush telegraph will be busy and what they don't know they'll invent.'

Alessandro shrugged, 'Do we care?'

'Not really, but you'll be a seven-day-wonder once it gets out Aunt Olivia is back.'

'This is a lovely place.' Alessandro stopped just before the harbour. Blue skies, a glittering silver sea and the lush green hills rising away from the village beyond the harbour. They walked to the inner harbour where fishermen were mending nets or cleaning out the boats ready to start for the day's catch.

Everyone greeted Jenna, but regarded

Alessandro with suspicion until Sam, already in his boat, called out that he was a visitor at Harbour View.

'Looks foreign to me,' muttered one, 'what's he doing with young Jenna — ain't she walking out with young Joshua Trethewey.'

Sam refused to comment further and started up his engine with a spluttering roar.

'Aren't strangers welcome?' Alessandro asked as his smiling greeting was met with surly nods at best, black looks at worst.

'Yes, but it takes a while. The fishermen are a close-knit lot. They have to get to know you.'

They were soon through the harbour and climbing the hill leading to the cliff path. The air was clear and pure and Alessandro took deep breaths, 'This is wonderful. I love Florence but sometimes the city smells are sometimes not so pleasant. You're lucky to live here.'

'Am I? I'm not so sure, I think I'd like to travel, I sometimes find life here claustrophobic, everyone knows every move you make. That's why I love to go out fishing with Dad, out at sea there aren't any boundaries . . . ' She stopped and looked towards the distant horizon, sharp-edged in the clear light.

Alessandro watched her profile, her hair failing over her shoulders. 'Come to Italy, there's much to see there.'

Jenna laughed, 'Not much chance of that.'

He put his hands on her shoulders, 'Why not? You're not bound here, you could travel, see the world and then be glad to return to your roots perhaps.' He held her gaze for a few seconds, his eyes looking deep into hers, 'You're a free spirit,' he gave her a little shake, 'I'll help you.'

She broke away, 'It's impossible, we're a poor family. We make a living but it's hard.'

'We are your family, Jenna, we can help each other.'

She stared at him and slowly her hand came to her mouth. 'We are

. . . cousins,' she said slowly, 'I've only just realised,' and her spirits sank as she knew she had to fight down the sweet sensations of his presence.

He looked stricken. 'You don't seem like a cousin.' For a while they walked together in silence.

As they rounded a corner a farm appeared, well back from the path. There was a stone house, several outbuildings and cattle in the fields being herded by a man and a young girl. They waved and Jenna waved back.

'Christine and her dad. She's my friend, I'll introduce you to them.' Glad of the diversion she walked across the fields towards them.

Alessandro looked around, 'Is there a road near here?'

'Why, yes, just beyond the house, the main road from the village towards Truro. It's quite new, it was just a track not long ago but what with more of the new motor cars now and some coaches it's quite busy.'

'And these buildings?' he queried.

'Dunno. George Polglaze used to rent out one of them, that square one set apart from the others near the road but there was some problem, a row. Ask him if you like.

'Jenna,' a tall shapely blonde girl gave Jenna a hug, 'good to see you. Come inside, Ma will be glad of some company. Dad, here's Jenna.'

'So I see,' he took off his cap and wiped his brow, 'and who's this fellow? Does Joshua know you're walking out with someone else?' He looked severely at Alessandro.

'I'm not walking out with Joshua,' Jenna said crossly, 'and Alessandro is my . . . ' she hesitated over the word but it had to be said, ' . . . cousin from Italy.

'Italy?' George looked as though she'd said 'from the moon'. 'Your cousin? Ah well now, welcome young man.' He held out his hand, 'Come inside, I'm parched, been milking since dawn. Mother will be pleased to see a new face. Italy you say?'

'Could I just ask,' Alessandro said,

'that building over there by the road, is it used?'

'I don't use it. Too far from the main buildings.'

'Could I look at it? Is it for rent?'

'Well, I dunno. Had some bother last time I rented it out. Why?'

'I'm not sure at the moment. It's just . . . I've an idea . . . and you have a dairy herd?'

'Yes — finest in the county. Top prizes at all the shows. Why?'

'Can I tell you later? It may come to nothing.'

Christine Polglaze was staring at Alessandro wide-eyed, 'Do please come into the farmhouse, Mother will love to meet you.' She took his arm and looked up at him, blue eyes sparkling.

Jenna's heart sank, she knew her friend, Christine well, and recognised the symptoms. Christine fell in and out of love with clockwork regularity and it was also her ambition to marry a rich man who would take her away from the drudgery of farm life.

# 5

Christine Polglaze watched her father and Alessandro cross the fields to the outbuildings before, wide-eyed, she turned back to Jenna. 'He's a find, Jen. Where did he come from?' She combed her fingers through her long blonde hair.

'I told you, Italy. He has business interests there.'

'What's he doing in Polgrehan?'

'He's brought his mother, my aunt Olive, and her granddaughter, Francesca, to visit.'

'Pretty name — Francesca, but you're a dark horse. Glamorous relatives suddenly turning up on your doorstep. It'll certainly give the village something to gossip about. I didn't even know you had an aunt. Maybe if I play it right your glamorous cousin could whisk me away to some romantic place in Italy. Wouldn't that be wonderful? You could come and visit. Is Alessandro rich?'

'Oh Christine, don't be silly. I don't suppose they'll stay here long, it's just a visit and I . . . '

Christine wasn't listening, she ran to open the door as the two men approached the farmhouse. 'Dad, can I get you some tea? You too, Alessandro?' She smiled at both but her eyes were glued to Alessandro.

'Get tea if you like for you and Jenna. Alessan . . . bit of a mouthful, I'll call you Alex — we want something stronger. Get out my scrumpy, we've something to celebrate.'

'Scrumpy?' Alessandro smiled at Christine.

'Dad's home-made cider, it's strong stuff — I shouldn't touch it if I were you. Ma'll be none too pleased to see you drinking it at this time of day.'

'You mind your manners girl, and do as you're told.'

'I . . . we ought to go,' Jenna said, 'I

promised Mum I wouldn't be long.'

'I think Aunt Mary will be glad to have time with her sister — and I should like to try this . . . er, scrumpy,' said Alessandro.

Christine put a flagon of cider on the table and poured out two tumblers.

'No, I really should be going.'

The men clinked glasses. 'To our deal,' George said and threw down a long swallow of the pale liquid.

Alessandro took a cautious sip and put his glass back on the table. 'Interesting,' he said diplomatically.

'An acquired taste,' Christine giggled, 'one that most folk round here acquire at birth. You'll see if you're here for the Fish Festival.'

'Fish Festival?'

'Highlight of Polgrehan's social calendar, the only one in fact. Village lets its hair down to celebrate the harvest of the sea. I can't think why, fish this year are scarce enough to keep you alive. Mainly it's just an excuse to get drunk and have a fight or two, or three. It's . . . '

'Will you stop jabbering girl,' her father rebuked, 'you've work to do. Your ma will expect dinner on the table when she's back from the church meeting.'

'And you'd better remove the scrumpy before she gets here,' retorted Christine, tossing her head.

'Mr Polglaze . . . George, our arrangement isn't final yet,' Alessandro said, 'it's pretty certain in my own mind but there's a lot of work to do if I'm to go ahead with my plan. I need to spend some time in Plymouth — that's your biggest town isn't it?'

'Depends what you're looking for. Plymouth's in Devon, across the River Tamar. Truro's nearer. I can see you're a good businessman and I'll be pleased to see that fellow Penhallorick put out of trade — thinks he owns the place.'

'That's not my aim,' Alessandro said in alarm, 'I'm not here to cause trouble. I've brought my mother to visit her native country, she may want to stay or to return to Italy but if I see a business opportunity I like to take it — and I'm sure there's one here.'

'But you'll stay a while?' Christine asked, eloquent blue eyes holding his. 'The deal with Father . . . '

'Not your business, you keep your mouth shut d'you hear.'

'We must go,' Alessandro interposed quickly, 'I have a lot to plan.'

George grunted, downed the last of his cider and took a gulp from Alessandro's untouched glass, 'And I'd best get back to the plough, but think on young man, if we do have a deal I want it tied up legal and proper, not like them other scoundrels . . . took advantage of my generosity.' Still muttering he grumbled his way back to his fields.

Christine waved Alessandro and Jenna goodbye, standing in the yard until they were well out of sight, wondering what she could wear for feast week, hoping and praying Alessandro would be in Polgrehan for the event.

Jenna and Alessandro walked back

along the cliff in silence for a while until Jenna could no longer contain her curiosity, 'So what is this thing with Mr Polglaze? You were ages looking at his buildings.'

'He took me over a couple of his fields but it's hard to make a decent living from it and he has no sons to help him carry on farming.'

'But why do you . . . ?' she persisted.

He stopped, took her arm and held her back beside him. 'Jenna, it's not a secret and I'll need your help, advice too, but I'd like to get a clear idea in my own head first before discussing it with the family. I've a business idea, maybe something for Mamma if she decides to stay here for a while. I have to go away for a few days, Plymouth or Truro, and then up to Scotland to trace my relatives there. I promise when I come back you'll hear my plans. All right?'

He smiled and Jenna's heart beat faster. She gasped and pressed her hand to her chest as though to slow the beat.

'Don't look so gloomy, Jenna,' he said

gently, 'you'll see, it'll turn out for the best. Mr Polglaze will be happy too if my plans work out. Your friend Christine is a charming girl. He's lucky to have such a daughter.'

'We were good friends at school.'

'And now?'

'We still meet but we're very different. She would love to leave the village, she's a town girl at heart really, longing to escape.'

'Are you?'

'No. I love Polgrehan and Cornwall. I'd miss the sea.'

'There are other seas.'

'I know. Maybe one day . . . ' she hesitated, it was none of her business but she was worried for him, he was a man of the cities, a foreigner too, who would know nothing of the undercurrents which could run in a small fishing village community like Polgrehan. She had to speak out, 'Alessandro, George Polglaze can be a difficult man. He's had trouble before over his buildings.'

'What sort of trouble? Are they about

to fall around his ears?'

'No, of course not, they've stood hundreds of years. Probably need some repairs.'

'That's not a problem, so what's wrong?'

'He used to rent his outbuildings before to certain men in the village.'

'So?'

'There was trouble, a quarrel, he threw them out, shut down the barns. They were very angry, they . . . they killed some of his livestock.'

'That's terrible — to harm animals. What was it all about?' Alessandro looked shocked.

'It was some years ago, it's sort of blown over although some people still won't speak to Mr Polglaze.'

'It must have been very important both to the men and George Polglaze.'

Jenna bit her lip, loyalty to her village ran strongly in her veins but, on the other hand, Alessandro was family and that loyalty came first. She had to speak, 'Round our coasts there used to be smugglers, many years ago, and there still are, though on a much smaller scale. The men who used Mr Polglaze's barn were smugglers, the barns were used to store contraband before it was distributed around the area. Mr Polglaze kept chickens there as cover. It worked well for years.'

'The police . . . your customs officers never discovered it?'

'Maybe, maybe not. Some would be bribed, some even part of it. It's more a game now, a game of wits and profit and many a blind eye's turned. The village of course is solidly behind the smugglers. I don't know a lot about it and I don't want to.' Jenna had a strong suspicion her father was involved in a peripheral way. When times were hard at home money would sometimes appear mysteriously after one of her dad's longer trips, trips which she obviously was barred from.

'Why did George Polglaze turn out those men?'

'I'm not sure. It's rumoured they

didn't always pay him, some say he got greedy and asked for too much. Others do say Martha Polglaze got wind of the smuggling and made him stop renting to the men. Strict Methodist is Martha and very much runs that household.'

'Well thanks, Jenna, I'll be very careful of Mr Polglaze and try to keep on the right side of Martha too.'

'I'm late,' she said quickly, 'I'm going on.' She started to run down the path to the village hoping he wouldn't catch her up. Once in the village she lingered over her shopping, chatting to anyone who had the time to spare. She didn't want to see Alessandro again just yet. She needed time to think.

As it happened when she returned to Harbour View he had already left and was not to return to Polgrehan for over a week. There was no word from him and her heart resumed its normal beat as she settled back into her normal routine.

Yet life had changed at Harbour View

since Olivia di Mascio and family had moved in. Seeing how tired and strained her younger sister was Olivia had, almost unnoticed, taken over the bulk of the guest house work.

Mary made no objections and gradually she relaxed, the taut coils in her mind easing and, to Sam's delight, he began to glimpse in rare flashes the young Mary he had loved and married. Olivia took over the cooking, introducing some Italian dishes. The guests loved it and business boomed.

Clarrie and Francesca were inseparable, so Mary had time to sit and talk to her sister while the two little girls played their games in the garden. Sam tended his chickens and his allotment, visiting The Three Pilchards without guilt as his wife's workload lightened.

But while there was harmony at Harbour View there were underlying tensions in Polgrehan itself. The news of Olive Kittow's return with her 'wrong-side-of-the-blanket-son' raised equal amounts of prejudice and tolerance. Strict chapel brethren condemned the sinner though the younger element didn't much care either way with a few exceptions, mainly members of the jilted Bert Trelawney family.

There old hurts and shame died hard. Now, with Polgrehans in two camps over the revival of the Olive Kittow scandal the latest rumours and gossip were fire to gunpowder.

Jenna always believed it was Christine Polglaze who, probably unwittingly, had started the rumour. Christine was a sharp girl who was very interested in Alessandro di Mascio's future. Only afterwards did Jenna recall a conversation they had on the beach. Christine had called on Jenna on some pretext or other, in reality she wanted news of Alessandro.

'Not back yet then?' she enquired as she and Jenna took the little girls down to the beach.

'No. I think he went to Scotland.'

'Ah, of course. Know when he's

back, he's been away over a week?'

'Is it that long? No, sorry, I've no idea.'

'Don't be sorry. I hear he's starting up a business in the village quite soon.'

'What?' Now she had Jenna's full attention.

'Business in the village — you heard.'

'It's news to me,' Jenna replied. 'How on earth did you know that?'

'I don't for sure, but I know he's renting the barns and fields from Dad. Well . . . I just happen to know there's a di Mascio family living in Scotland . . . and . . . '

'Get on, do.'

'Their business is in ice-cream, they make it, sell it in their ice-cream parlours and round the towns by horse and cart. Horses d'you see? Need fields. Making ice-cream you need a factory. Horses, fields, barns — all fits doesn't it?'

'But there's already an ice-cream parlour — Jim Penhallorick, and he sells round the village. Alessandro said he didn't want to cause trouble in the village. Who else knows about this — if it's true?'

'I really don't know,' Christine laid out her towel on the soft sand, 'anyway it means he'll be here for a while and that's nice for you isn't it, to have your cousin here? Plus your auntie.' She stretched out her body to the sun and closed her eyes. 'Keep your eyes on the little ones, Jen, tide's on the turn and going out now.'

Jenna shaded her eyes from the sun, Clarrie and Francesca were too near the water's edge. She shouted to them and they came to her laughing and giggling, pulling her round until she couldn't help but join in their game.

'Christine, I'm going in now, it's tea time. You coming in for tea?'

'I'd like to,' Christine sat up, 'but I'll stay here for a while. The sun's lovely and I need a few things in the village. I'll see you later.'

Jenna hesitated, she should warn Christine not to spread rumours about

Alessandro, it would only cause trouble. Surely she wouldn't want to stir up trouble for Alessandro? But Christine was a bit of a gossip . . .

As she dithered the girls started to run back towards the sea. 'No, no, here — at once.' She ran after them and forgot about her friend on the beach but as she gathered up the girls the thoughts in her head couldn't be pushed aside.

If it was true what Christine had said, that Alessandro would be involved in the village and life at Harbour View, then this was a bitter-sweet blow to Jenna. Her feelings for Alessandro became clearer by the day, feelings she had to suppress. The only way she could do that was to leave Harbour View herself even if it meant taking a live-in job with the Poultners at the Hall.

# 6

The summer season began with the fine weather bringing a bumper crop of visitors to Cornwall. Business was brisk at Harbour View and Olivia had just finished the breakfast cooking when the telegraph boy knocked on the front door.

'Oh my!' Mary took the telegraph gingerly. 'It's for you, Olive. Not bad news I hope?'

Olivia opened the yellow envelope and scanned the brief message. 'No, it's fine. From Alessandro, he's coming back this evening. He says . . . '*successful conclusion, arrive late p.m. Thursday by motor van!*''

'Alessandro knows what he's doing, you mustn't worry. So, what shall we cook for his supper, pasties or a bit of fresh bass. There are plenty of fish in the store.'

'Let's have both,' Sam called from the back porch where he was cleaning his garden tools. 'I'll nip out for some ale. Could be a bit of a celebration from the sound of it.'

Mary raised her eyebrows. 'Any excuse.' But she said it kindly and with a smile for her husband.

'Do you miss Italy, Aunt Olivia?' Jenna came in with a tray of dirty crocks from the guests' dining-room.

'Some things, of course. Santini was my home for over a quarter of a century but Polgrehan's in my blood too. It's . . . it WAS my home . . . '

'So,' Jenna prompted, 'are you happy here?'

Her aunt carefully washed a pile of plates before answering. 'I love the village, but it's awkward. When I go out I feel I'm being watched . . . talked about. I sense disapproval and I know I'm not forgiven.'

Sam came in for his jacket. 'I think there are a few who hold a grudge, who won't let the past die but there are lots who speak of you kindly and are glad to see you back, happy with your son and grandchild. I do have the ear of the village perhaps more than Jenna or Mary.'

'I hope you're right, Sam, but I shouldn't trespass on your hospitality much longer. Maybe we should rent a place of our own.'

'I shan't hear of it,' Mary said firmly, 'and we shouldn't decide anything until we know what Alessandro's plans are.'

Jenna found it hard to concentrate that morning. She had rooms to clean, beds to change for new guests, tasks she normally whizzed through, but this morning she found herself standing by the window, staring at the distant horizon, clean sheets over her arm, her mind well away from Harbour View. Soon Alessandro would arrive and her heart would quicken its beat however much she scolded it. Finally with a sigh, she gave herself a mental shake, made up the beds and polished the rooms to shining perfection.

Downstairs she found her mother and aunt deep in preparation for Alessandro's return with a grand family supper to greet him. 'Anything I can do?' she asked.

'Not really,' Mary replied. 'Why don't you take the girls to the beach. It's a lovely day.'

The brilliant early summer day relaxed and calmed Jenna as she concentrated on teaching dark-haired Francesca basic swim strokes. Clarrie couldn't help showing off. She was a natural water baby but she was kind and encouraging too, to her young cousin. They splashed, picnicked and played on the sand until the golden sun grew large and began to roll westwards.

Jenna started to pack up. 'Gather all your things,' she called to the girls, holding out a beach bag, but they simply dropped their wet things on the sand and raced past her, arms outstretched.

'Uncle Aless, Uncle Aless,' they chanted as he scooped them up, one on each arm. 'Fran, Clarrie.' He hugged them before he walked more slowly to Jenna.

She pushed back her dark curls and took deep breaths to still her thudding heart. 'Alessandro, I'm glad to see you back.'

He knelt to stand the girls on the sand. 'Are you, Jenna? Truly?'

'Of course. We're all longing to hear your news. How was the trip?' She was proud of the casual way she managed to speak and control the breathless excitement that welled up at the sight of him.

'Let's go in then.' He held out his hands to the small girls. 'And I'll tell you all about it.'

Some hours later when the guests had been fed and the sleepy girls tucked up top-to-tail in Clarrie's bed, Alessandro told them his plans. Rob and Sam had already admired the smart maroon motor van parked outside, gold lettering picking out the logo of '*di Mascio's finest ice-cream*'. Now they all silently read a summary sheet of Alessandro's business plan. It was several minutes before anyone said anything.

'So you're all set to go.' Sam was the first to speak. 'This is very impressive, you must have worked twenty hours a day.'

Alessandro laughed. 'Not really. I've had lots of help from our relatives in Scotland. They're doing well up there and I just followed their advice and business plans. They're expanding and buying new equipment so they're sending down lots of second-hand machinery.'

'And the factory — Polglaze Farm?' Olivia queried.

'All in hand. George got things moving. I'm employing Christine Polglaze, and the equipment from Scotland will be here in a few days.'

'I don't know a great deal about business,' Sam said, 'but it looks good to me. One thing though I must tell you. There have been rumours in Polgrehan. I don't know how, but the word got around that Jim Penhallorick is up in arms about you setting up a rival business and so are some of the more hide-bound who resent any change especially if those changes are made by . . . er . . . '

'Foreigners,' Alessandro helped him out. 'But my mother is Cornish born, of Polgrehan.'

'Yes, but . . . ' Mary was silenced by Sam's warning glance.

'My past reputation,' Olive spoke sadly. 'One of 'my sort' is beyond the pale, I've forfeited my village rights.'

'That's not true.' Jenna was quick to disagree.

'Mamma need not be involved at all,' Alessandro said quickly, 'and I'm not setting up in the village. It's too small. I want to open up in a large resort up the coast, and the factory is to be on Mr Polglaze's land, so I can't see a problem there. It's way out of the village.'

'But, I . . . It's . . . ' Sam burst out, then abruptly stopped.

'A problem?' Alessandro frowned.

'No.' But Sam looked worried and Jenna thought she knew why.

'I should like to involve all my family,' Alessandro continued.

'Count me out,' Sam said hastily. 'No head for business, enough irons in the fire.'

'So I thought.' Alessandro nodded. 'Rob? Jenna?'

'How could we help?' Rob asked.

'You could start by selling on the road, horse and cart to start, maybe later one of the motor vans.'

'Gosh, I'd like that. Would I make enough money for my own boat one day?'

'No reason why not. Our ice-cream will be magnificent, I promise you — a wonderful seller.'

'Count me in, and Matt, too when he hears, I'm sure.'

'Jenna?'

'I . . . I don't know . . . ' Visions of working with Christine and Alessandro together dismayed her. 'There's Mother — if Aunt Olivia is working for you up the coast, maybe . . . '

'I can do both,' Olivia interrupted. 'I

love to work, it's what I'm used to and . . . ' She looked round with a shy smile. 'I can drive to and fro in one of the di Mascio vans.'

Mary gasped. 'You drive? A motor car!'

'It's not that unusual, Angelo taught me. I used to collect the supplies for the trattoria. I love driving, it would be no problem helping my sister and helping to manage the di Mascio ice-cream business.'

In the following silence they all explored the ramifications of Alessandro's bombshell. He'd flung a huge stone, the ripples had to be absorbed. It was Mary who got up first. 'Pasties are ready, and I'll put the fish to fry.' Her voice shook a little as she said, 'I'm all for it, it'll be a real challenge.' She reached up to kiss Alessandro. 'I can't do much myself but I'll support you all the way, it's just what this family needs. You, Rob, and Jenna, you make your own decisions but I'll support you too.'

Sam gasped, took a swig of ale, went

to kiss his wife. 'Well done, love, that's like my old sweetheart.' He went to shake hands with Alessandro. 'Good luck to you too, you deserve to succeed.'

Rob gave a whoop and picked up his beer glass. 'Here's to us!'

Alessandro was rather taken aback by the enthusiasm he'd generated. He knew he'd taken a chance by setting the wheels in motion before consulting the family but he wasn't ready to return to Italy yet. Strong ties were binding him to Cornwall though he could not yet admit the true reason. He looked at Jenna. 'And you?'

'I . . . I'm not sure.' She knew she should say no. It was courting heart-break to throw in her lot with Alessandro but she so desperately wanted to do something different, to take up the challenge, to succeed at something in her life. It was such an opportunity. It was madness too, but she looked him in the eyes and nodded.

It all happened with lightning speed.

The summer season still had weeks to go when the di Mascio ice-cream carts began to appear in the highways and lanes of the county, and at many summer fetes, shows and fairs. The factory at Polglaze Farm was working flat out and a smart new ice-cream parlour was thriving at Caltarrick, a growing resort on the North Cornwall coast.

Alessandro took on more and more staff and Olivia seemed to be in all places at once though she told her son, 'My priority is to my sister, she comes first you must understand.'

'I do, Mamma,' he'd replied and simply hired more staff to place at points of need. His energy was tremendous, his was the overall view and it left him with little spare time.

Jenna could hardly believe the change in her life. She worked long hours and would turn her hand to anything from helping to make the ice-cream to packing the ice for the ice-cream carts, to keeping accounts of expenses and takings. She learned as she went along and she learned quickly.

Christine too had a new lease of life — she would never know by what magic Alessandro had persuaded Martha Polglaze that her daughter would be a valuable asset to the di Mascio business. Perhaps it was the regular and good wage he promised to pay. Christine would have happily worked a twelve-hour day for nothing to gain Alessandro's notice and approval.

One evening after a busy holiday weekend, Jenna was at the factory in the tiny office she used for her paperwork. Absorbed in figures and invoices, she was startled by a car door slamming outside.

'Jenna.' Alessandro came into the room. 'What on earth are you doing? It'll be dark soon. You should be home.'

'I didn't notice the time go by. I was . . . '

'Whatever it was, it can wait until morning. I'm taking you home, the van's outside.'

'I'd rather walk.'

'I'll walk with you.'

'But your van's here.'

'No matter, I'll walk back in the morning.'

The air was balmy, dusk gathering, the heat of the day giving way to the slight sharpness in the air that heralded season change. They fell into step, side by side. Alessandro held her arm as she stumbled over a stone but quickly released her.

'Aren't you tired?' she asked. 'You've worked so hard these past weeks.'

'I find it exhilarating. Don't you?'

'In a way but what will happen in the winter when the tourists have gone home?'

'The hotels stay open all year, and we'll consolidate on these last weeks.'

They walked in silence until the harbour lights of Polgrehan shone below. 'It's a pretty sight,' he said softly.

'Yes it is.' Jenna felt his closeness like a fire and she drew away.

He took her hand.

'No . . .'

'Jenna, I know. I want to say — it's hard, but we'll survive. I shall move out of Harbour View. Mamma and Francesca will stay. But . . . near you . . . it's so hard and . . . '

She put a finger on his lips. 'Don't say anything. We work together, that's all it can ever be.'

He sighed. 'I can't believe . . . It doesn't feel like . . . '

'Please, Alessandro, no more. I'm enjoying the work, don't spoil it for me. You'll find someone . . . '

'I don't want . . . ' He took her hand, raised it to his lips, then let it go. 'I'm going back to the factory. Can you walk on from here?'

'Of course. Goodnight, Alessandro.'

'Goodnight, Jenna.'

Meanwhile, Polgrehan watched the rising fortunes of the di Mascios with mixed feelings. Jim Penhallorick and his cronies were dead set against the venture for more secret and sinister reasons than simple jealousy of Alessandro's commercial success, but on the whole they were in a minority.

A growing number of villagers welcomed the di Mascio venture. It gave much needed jobs to the young people who found it a novelty and the older folk were reminded of the prosperous years of the pilchard fishing and canning industry, when Polgrehan had enjoyed full employment with a strong community spirit.

Gradually the success of the venture rubbed off on Olivia. People admired her hard work and the way she'd pulled her sister out of her deepening depression. When they heard how she lost her daughter, Marietta, in childbirth, their sympathy was fully engaged.

As the summer drew to a close, Alessandro called in his staff one Friday evening to pay out overtime bonuses and congratulate all concerned. There was a party atmosphere and a feeling of relaxation and relief that the first summer season had been a good one and the new venture was set to carry on in the future.

'Gig race and Fish Festival to round it all off,' Rob said to Alessandro.

'Gig? I've heard of the Fish Festival but not the gig races. Tell me.'

'Gigs — Cornish row boats,' Christine joined in. 'Six rowers and cox, going since the 1790s. They used to take the harbour pilot out to the sailing ships, later used for smuggling, or lifeboats.'

'Used for racing now,' Joe Edwards, one of the ice-cream cart sellers, put in eagerly. 'There's a sort of league table between villages. Polgrehan's near the top of the league though Scilly Island teams usually win. Not this year though. Tomorrow's the final, us and Tresedder. We'll all be there tomorrow, so you must come down to the harbour, Alessandro.

'Why don't we take an ice-cream cart down to the harbour?' Joe said. 'I bet we'd sell a brave lot. Weather forecast's hot for tomorrow.'

'I can't help,' Rob said. 'I'm in the team — but everyone turns out for the gig racing.'

'Then I'd better join them.' Alessandro laughed.

The following day Polgrehan Harbour was a sight to behold. Bunting was strung across the narrow streets, fishing boats in the inner harbour were decked out with flags and by midday the streets around the harbour were packed with locals, visitors and gig enthusiasts. Jenna, her mother and aunt were in the crowd on the harbour and Sam was one of the race marshals. Jenna saw Christine hanging on to Alessandro's arm as they struggled through the crowd.

The gigs, 32 feet long, made of Cornish elm, held seats for six rowers and a cox. The Tresedder gig was in the water ready to go, the Polgrehan gig still on land. Sam and Rob were conferring with the team, looking worried.

'What's up?' Mary craned her neck to see.

'Dunno.'

'There are only five rowers.' Jenna

leapt on to a crate to see what was happening. 'I think they're a rower short. Chris Sampson's not there — he's the missing member.'

Sam addressed the crowds through a loudhailer. 'Emergency here. Chris Sampson's been in a tractor accident. He's all right, patched up in hospital, but now we're one man short for the Polgrehan gig. Any reserves out there?'

There was some commotion but no action.

'They've had trouble finding a team all year,' Jenna told Olivia, 'and if they can't find someone, Tresedder takes the cup by default.'

'For goodness' sake,' Mary groaned, 'there must be someone.'

'Alessandro can row, he has trophies at home,' Olivia said.

After several minutes, the Tresedder marshal looked at his watch and mimed to the crowd, 'Race lost if Polgrehan fails to produce a full team.'

Several young lads jostled forward but they were too young, without the mature strength and stamina needed to speed the gigs out of the harbour to the buoy and back twice. The Tresedder team began to slow-handclap. Their coach held up three fingers. 'Three minutes . . . '

'Here!' yelled Christine Polglaze and pushed Alessandro forward. He protested, Christine said something to the crowd and they immediately pushed him toward the gig. He shook his head and tried to hang back but now Sam spoke to him and then turned to the Tresedder coach. 'Alessandro di Mascio, son of Polgrehan born and bred Olive Kittow, gold medallist in the local Italian regattas. He qualifies.'

Both teams looked in amazement as Alessandro was practically pushed down the harbour steps and into the waiting gig.

Jenna watched, hand over her mouth as Alessandro splashed his oar and seemed awkward with the stroke. The cox bent to say something to him, Alessandro nodded, found the rhythm and the Polgrehan gig shot away in front of Tresedder's.

It was the most exciting race anyone had remembered for years. First Polgrehan, then Tresedder pulled ahead. Neck and neck they raced in the final return to the harbour. Tresedder nosed in front, yards away from the harbour entrance, then with a mighty effort, the Polgrehan boat widened the gap between them and touched home seconds before Tresedder.

Panting, the men bent over their oars, but with one accord, the Polgrehan crew reached out to Alessandro to pat him on the shoulder before giving the thumbs-up to the cheering crowd.

'Well,' Mary was almost dancing with excitement, 'that does it. Alessandro is the hero of the day. No-one can say he's not one of us now.'

Jenna cheered too but her heart sank as she saw Christine meet Alessandro from the gig. She threw her arms round his neck and kissed him and he kissed her back.

What the cheering crowd didn't see was Joe Edwards in the back streets of Polgrehan, preparing to return to base after a successful sell-out of di Mascio ice-cream. Trundling his empty cart up the hill, he was set upon by several men, jostled to the ground, and his cart up-ended on top of him before the men vanished.

# 7

It was several days before the excitement of the gig race died down but the village was busy, the last week of the season attracted many visitors to the popular Fish Festival. The di Mascio business was still operating at full stretch, Joe Edwards told the police he'd stumbled and fallen, pulling the cart on top of him. Nobody believed him but he was stubborn and the police shelved the case although everyone though they knew the culprits.

Jenna tried to keep occupied and was happy to spend hours at the factory, except for Christine's constant chatter about Alessandro, 'what he'd said to her', 'did Jenna think her cousin was attracted to her', 'should Christine ask him to go to the Fish Festival with her', 'wasn't he the most attractive man in the village', 'so superior to any of the locals'? And so on and on until Jenna longed to scream at her to stop and began to think once again of leaving the village altogether and look for a job in a neighbouring town.

But she loved the work, every aspect of it, loved to see the paddling of milk and sugar in the huge round wooden tubs and the addition of what Alessandro called the secret di Mascio ingredients known only to the family.

She enjoyed serving there too, making ice-cream sundaes, banana splits and knickerbockers glories. The parlour at Caltarrick was a wonderful escape from Christine's romantic ramblings and her own heartache.

As the day of the Fish Festival approached Christine confided she'd asked Alessandro to accompany her and he'd agreed.

Jenna was late home for tea, her mother had set her plate in the oven to keep warm. 'You look tired,' Mary said worriedly, 'it's the job — too much for you and for Olive too. She'd hardly finished her tea before she rattled off in her van to Caltarrick — staff shortage there she said.'

'I think we're both enjoying it. I worry about you though. Are you managing?'

'I am. I've a new lease of life since Olive and her son and granddaughter came here. I'd become a miserable old biddy before they came, hadn't I?'

'You've had a great deal to do but I'm glad you feel happier now.' Jenna kissed her mother, 'And you're not a miserable old biddy!'

'I do hope Olive stays, I've grown to depend on her, and Clarrie would be miserable if Francesca goes.'

'I didn't think they're going anywhere just yet,' Jenna pushed her plate away, the food barely touched, 'Alessandro is too committed to the di Mascio business right now.'

'I hear Christine Polglaze has set her cap at him . . . Jenna, what's wrong with your tea?'

'I'm not hungry, Mum. I'm sorry.'

A knock at the door interrupted them. 'Oh Jenna I forgot to tell you, that's probably Josh Trelawney, he called earlier. Your aunt opened the door and he fled like a jack rabbit. Said he'd call again.'

Jenna got up wearily, she was tired but had thought an evening swim would pep her up. She didn't particularly want to see Josh, but then why not? Maybe he would stop her thinking of Alessandro. She was fond of Josh, a companion since they were toddlers together and when she opened the door she felt a rush of affection for his tall figure with its unruly mop of dark-blond hair. 'Josh, good to see you. It's been ages.'

'You've been pretty busy yourself. Can you come out tonight?'

'Yes, I'd like to. What shall we do?'

'Don't mind. It's hot enough for a swim, there's the usual gang down by the harbour. We can have a drink in the café after — or a walk.'

'A swim would be nice, I'll get my things.'

It was fun in the harbour, she hadn't realised how much she'd missed during these last weeks. Since the di Mascio business started she'd hardly set foot in the village let alone swim in the sea or the harbour, the harbour summer evening swims being the social centre for the young people of Polgrehan.

She and Josh joined in an impromptu game of water polo before racing each other across the harbour mouth, skilfully avoiding the many fishing and holiday crafts returning to base at the end of the day.

Finally, as the sun set, they climbed up the steps from the water and on to the quayside. They sat with their friends on the sun-warmed stone walls of the jetty and dried off. She combed her fingers through her wet hair and squinted at the blazing red sun about to be swallowed by the horizon. 'Thanks, Josh, I enjoyed that. Almost forgotten what fun was like.'

'Working too hard for that di Mascio fellow. You should get out more.'

'Probably right, but I enjoy the work. Really. It's pretty new so it's exciting. Nothing much happened around here before they came.'

'You used to like it before.' Josh rubbed his hair so hard it fairly crackled.

'I still do — and you haven't been around much either.'

'I couldn't, I . . . not with . . . not with them around.'

'Who?' Jenna asked knowing full well who he meant.

'di Mascio and his . . . her, you know.'

Jenna stopped combing her hair and grabbed the towel from Josh. 'Who's HER? What's wrong? Do you mean my aunt, Olivia di Mascio and her son and granddaughter?'

'That's the one, Olive Kittow. How she's the nerve to come back here.'

'What's it to do with you, Josh Trelawney? Oh God, Josh — your Uncle Bert?'

'My Uncle Bert. Course, I never knew him and until recently never knew what killed him. My Aunt Agatha told me, his older sister.'

'Bert Trelawney was killed in the Great War surely.'

'Yes, but why did he join up? He didn't need to did he? Farmer — reserved occupation. He went because your aunt broke his heart, left him at the altar for that foreigner, carrying his baby too. I never knew about it until she — your aunt, came back, and what for — to cause more trouble?'

'Oh Josh, of course she's not come to cause trouble, but I'm sorry, I didn't know about it either until they came, but surely you don't still bear a grudge — your family?'

Josh pulled on his shirt, pushed his feet into his shoes and looked Jenna in the eye, 'Well, I suppose I don't, not really, but Aunt Aggie's upset, brought it all back even though she's very old now. She remembers it like yesterday. Bert was a late baby and she more or

121

less brought him up, grieved a lot when he was killed.'

'I'm sorry,' Jenna said again and put her arms round him, 'truly sorry, but Aunt Olivia's paid the price, she lost her daughter in childbirth and her home in Santini is ruined — a volcano erupted and devastated her village.' Impulsively she drew Josh's face to hers and kissed him. He tasted of salt and seaweed and he pulled her into his arms. She drew away just in time to see Christine and Alessandro walking along the top wall of the harbour towards the jetty.

Jenna looked away but Christine called down to them, 'Jenna, Josh, been swimming? Lovely evening.' She waved and linked her arm possessively in Alessandro's.

Jenna and Josh sat in silence for a while. 'So will you meet my Aunt Olivia sometime?' Jenna asked gently.

Josh sighed, 'I suppose so, everyone else has and he . . . her son seems mighty popular, especially since the gig race.'

'He didn't want to do that, Christine pushed him into it.'

'He did well, but there's still some don't take to him. They're jealous of his success and there are mutterings in some quarters. That incident with Joe Edwards was no accident. So a friendly warning. The Trelawneys are a civilised lot and might bury the hatchet, forgive and forget, but there's some won't let go of an old grudge and others who couldn't care one way or the other will exploit that grudge.'

'What are you talking about? It's getting chilly. Come on, let's go for a drink. I'll pay.'

'No and won't, AND I'm not coming unless you promise you'll come to the Fish Festival with me.'

'I may be working . . . '

'No you won't Joe told me you've all got a day off — unless anyone wants to work, which Joe does of course.'

'Why does he?'

'He's getting married in a few weeks to Edna Benett, needs the overtime.'

'All right, it's a deal, you say hello nicely to my Aunt Olivia and I'll come with you to the Fish Festival. Only in the evening mind, I've too much to do at work in the morning and I promised Francesca and Clarrie I'd take them to the fair in Alley Fields in the afternoon.'

Josh put his hands on her shoulders, drew her to him and kissed her, 'We are friends aren't we, Jen?'

'Of course,' she said briskly, standing up and brushing sand from her clothes, 'haven't we always been?'

Fish Festival — the final celebration of the season, originally a thanksgiving service for the harvest of the sea, now an excuse for a day's partying in the last of the summer sunshine before the autumn church harvest festivals blessed the produce of the land.

There was a morning service at the Methodist chapel to give spiritual thanks, then a start to the real fun which was purely secular — decorated floats and a procession through the streets to the harbour where the

Fishermens' Queen would be chosen and crowned and then lead her court around the harbour to the traditional Floral Dance thumped out by the town band. There was a bit of a lull in the afternoon when the children went up to the fair in Alley Fields on the cliffs.

In the evening the grand finale, a mammoth fish barbecue on the quay; ale and provisions, fish and all, donated by Lord and Lady Poultner from the big house.

The Three Pilchards was crowded, tempers began to fray as the bar staff worked furiously to satisfy the demand for ever more ale. When Jenna and Josh went in for a drink after listening to the band, the atmosphere was thick with smoke, glasses were being knocked to the floor and the noise was ear-shattering.

Jenna coughed, 'Too crowded.'

'I'll get us a drink and we'll take it outside.' Josh pushed his way through the crowd.

'Jenna,' Rob and Matthew came over.

'Hi, what a crush. Good to see you, Matt. How's life at the Hall?'

He pulled a face, 'Not keen. Rob's persuading me to join di Mascio's.'

'Really?'

Her brother nodded, 'He's brought me here to meet Alessandro. Once we see him we'll go somewhere quieter.'

'Over there, with Christine Polglaze, by the window. Come and join us, Jenna.'

'I'm waiting for Josh. We'll come over, but it's hopeless in here, we're going outside. Meet you there.'

But they never did get their drinks outside and Jenna was never quite sure how it all started. Through the smoke she saw three men, older men not of the village, sitting at a table, tankards well primed. As Rob and Matt approached Alessandro and Christine one of the men nudged the others, pointed to Alessandro and Jenna heard the words 'Jezebel' quite clearly.

All three then stared pointedly at Alessandro, he frowned, started to say something, but Christine put her hand on his arm and he turned away to greet Rob and Matt. The three men looked at each other and nodded. One stood up, tapped Alessandro on the shoulder and said loudly, 'So you're the Kittow by-blow.'

After that Jenna could only recall a blur, Alessandro leapt at the man and with one blow felled him to the ground. For a split second there was dead silence then the other two men knocked him to the ground, kicking him viciously. Rob and Matt moved to pull them off, Josh hesitated, looked back at Jenna and launched into the attack to help Alessandro.

After that it was a matter of flying fists, chairs and tables knocked over, the landlord roaring for calm and screams from the women. Jenna was pinned against the bar counter, struggled for breath until someone lifted the counter flat and pulled her to the safety of the other side of the bar.

'Get the police,' the landlord yelled

to the girl who'd pulled Jenna to safety, 'don't just stand there and watch, PICK UP THE PHONE!'

Jenna watched horrified as the fight rolled around her. Then she saw Alessandro was trying to get Christine out of the door, but she had picked up a walking stick and was belabouring a huge burly man with it, yelling as she did so.

Suddenly the door burst open and three policemen charged into the room laying about them with truncheons and at once the fight stopped as suddenly as it had begun.

'Evening constables,' the landlord beamed, wiping blood from his chin, 'any problems?'

The sergeant sighed, 'We've been sitting in the station expecting your call any minute, we've asked for reinforcements from town. This looks nastier than usual. Who started it now?'

Swiftly the chaos turned to order as people resumed their seats, picked up any glasses still standing and peered innocently into their empty depths. The sergeant got out his notebook and with very little hope began questioning people. Nobody knew anything, nothing had happened, perhaps a little argument here and there — feast day, what do you expect? 'Mr di Mascio, I didn't expect you to be involved in this, can you tell me what happened?'

'No, just a quiet drink here with friends.' Christine clung to his arm, Matt and Rob somehow had full tankards.

'Nothing to worry about, sergeant,' Rob said.

Tension eased once the police had gone, the landlord served one last drink to those who needed it then called 'time' and hustled everyone out into the night.

It was crowded on the quay as people dispersed and somehow in the darkness Jenna and Alessandro became separated from the others. 'Jenna, are you all right?' Alessandro said urgently.

'I'm fine, but you must be hurt. What happened?'

'I'm not hurt, but that was deliberate — those men talking about us, about my mother — there's anger and hatred here. It's all my fault, I shouldn't have come.'

'No, no, please, you mustn't think of leaving. It's only a few people and . . .' she bit her lip.

'Jenna,' she heard Josh calling.

'I must go, and Alessandro, I can't work for you any more . . . it's . . . it's too painful . . . you and Christine . . .'

'Jenna,' he grabbed her arm, 'please, you mustn't leave, there's nothing between me and Christine. I should go . . .'

'No . . . my mother . . . Rob . . . they're so much happier. I shall get a job up at the Hall and it'll be easier if I don't see you any . . .'

'Jenna,' he pulled her to him roughly, 'you can't . . .' His lips found hers in a crushing kiss.

'Jenna?' Josh was nearer.

She broke free, 'I'm so sorry, Alessandro . . . ' She ran towards where Josh was calling her.

'Jen, you all right? I was worried, I missed you.'

'I'm fine.' She looked back and saw Christine holding on to Alessandro who was looking over her head towards where Jenna had disappeared.

It was then that Jenna knew definitely that she had to put as much distance as possible between herself and Alessandro di Mascio.

# 8

The day following the Fish Festival was a Sunday. Jenna woke at dawn, crept out of Harbour View and walked up to the Polglaze Farm factory. She spent a couple of hours clearing her paperwork and left a note for Christine to tell her she was leaving di Mascio's. For Alessandro she left a sealed note which said simply, *'I have to go. You must understand. I'm sorry.'*

She was back in time to help with breakfasts and get the little girls ready for Sunday School. She knew Alessandro would be at Caltarrick all day, he took the Sunday shift to give his mother a completely free day to spend with granddaughter, Francesca, and sister, Mary. They usually all went to chapel where feeling towards Olivia was softening by the week.

'Pleased to see you both here again,'

the new young preacher said, 'you are very welcome and I hope you'll stay in Polgrehan for a good long while.' His words were balm to Olivia and she began to feel she really had come home.

Jenna took the girls to the beach on Sunday afternoon and continued Francesca's swimming lessons. To her surprise Olivia joined them for a picnic tea. 'Your ma's having a lie down and Sam's out fishing,' she explained, 'so I thought I'd see how Francesca's doing with her swimming.'

'Coming on fine.' Jenna called out to the girls, 'Come and have a race. Fran, show your mum what you can do. With a ten yards start Francesca took an early lead as they swam parallel to the beach but Clarrie caught up and just won by a body's length. 'See, she'll soon be ready for the harbour swims,' Jenna laughed as the girls plunged back into the surf.

'You've done wonders with her,' Olivia was impressed.

'I enjoy it.'

Olivia picked up handfuls of soft sand, 'I was so happy here when I was young,' she said softly, 'I never thought I'd come back again . . . but after all it was the right thing to do.'

'I'm glad you came back. Mother is so much better.'

'And you, Jenna, are you happy?'

Jenna looked away. 'See the girls, do you think they're too far out?'

'Hardly, only a yard or two off the shore. You didn't answer my question.'

'Of course I'm happy but . . . ' she hesitated, Aunt Olivia had to know of course but it was hard to find a plausible explanation. 'Er . . . I'm leaving di Mascio's,' she blurted out, 'I . . . think I need a change.'

'A change? I don't understand, surely di Mascio's is a change. I thought you loved the work.'

'I do, I did, but I've been thinking — I ought not to be tied to . . . to the family. I mean, it might not work out . . . '

'Alessandro will be upset, he relies on

you, you've a real head for business. Can't you stay with us?'

Jenna shook her head, 'I've made up my mind, Christine can do my work, I've left it tidy and . . .'

'Already!' Olivia couldn't hide her astonishment.

'It's best . . . look, those girls are far too far out. I'll fetch them back.' She ran off leaving Olivia di Mascio with a very puzzled frown on her face.

On Monday morning Jenna was up once again at dawn. She left a note for her parents saying she'd gone up to the Hall and had left di Mascio's. That way she hoped to avoid the inevitable questioning. She was taking a chance that Lady Dorothy would be at home and would see her straight away.

Fred Took, the butler, who was a friend of her father, answered the door, 'Why, Jenna, what're you doing here? I saw you coming up the drive. Nothing wrong at Harbour View I hope.'

'No, everyone's fine. I'd like to see Lady Dorothy if that's possible.'

'I'll see what I can do. What's it about?'

'I . . . I need a job.'

'A job? But I . . . we all thought the Pascoes had joined di Mascio's. Young Rob's gone, Matt to follow apparently.'

'Well . . . '

'You don't have to explain to me.' He pulled a face, 'Never works, working for the family. I've not spoken to my brother these past ten years because of a fall out over Dad's blacksmithing business.' He shook his head slowly. 'Come in and wait — through there, that's her office, you might have a bit of a wait, she's giving Cook her orders for the week.' He bent to whisper in Jenna's ear, 'Bark's worse than her bite, you just stand up to her, she'll like that.'

He showed Jenna into an office, a large room overlooking a wide sweep of lawn which sloped down to a thick wood. She went to the wide bay window to admire the view: blue sea glittered beyond the treetops to the distant horizon.

'Jenna Pascoe?'

Jenna spun round. 'Lady Poultner, I'm sorry, I was admiring the view.'

'Don't be sorry, I frequently admire it. Do sit down. Took tells me you are after a job.' Lady Dorothy's aristocratic features reflected her noble birth, a woman of formidable energy she had restored Poultner Hall to former glory, bringing wealth and brains into the somewhat dissolute Poultner line. She eyed Jenna keenly. 'I seem to remember your mother enquiring via Took about a parlour maid position for you some weeks ago.'

'I believe she did, yes.'

'Is that what you want to do?'

Jenna bit her lip. It wasn't. So why was she here? 'I'll be honest, Lady Dorothy, I'm looking for a change. I need . . . I would like to live away from home for a while.'

'Don't you get on with your family?'

'I do, but . . . '

'No need for explanation. I heard that you and other members of your family had joined the new di Mascio business. Doing well I believe. But it doesn't suit you apparently?'

'No, not for the moment.'

'You did the paperwork?'

'Among other things, yes.'

Lady Dorothy shuffled some papers on her desk, looking up once or twice at Jenna who remained calm, waiting for further developments. Lady Dorothy finally said abruptly, 'There isn't a position here for a parlour maid. What I need is a personal assistant.'

She pointed to a pile of papers, 'I do a lot of charity work in the county and I have a busy social life. As you see my energies aren't channelled into the paperwork. I find it very tedious, I feel you could be useful to me and I've heard good things about your work at di Mascio's.'

'How . . . ?'

'Never mind now — not much in the village gets by without my notice. So, you'll take it on?'

'Well, it's a little . . . '

'Good, so that's settled: flexible

working hours, live in or out according to what's needed, start right away, you can begin on this lot, there's more in the filing cabinet. Make yourself known to Molly, the cook and Lois, the housekeeper — you'll need to liaise with them. We have to give a lot of dinner parties — fund-raising you see.' She stood up, shook Jenna's hand and walked briskly out of the office.

The next few days seemed unreal, Jenna made a start on Lady Dorothy's chaotic paper work, enjoying sorting out her engagement diary and filing information on her various and numerous charitable causes. She had her own bed sitting room, a blessing as she used it as an excuse to escape the baffled questioning of her family, and Christine.

Autumn was a busy time; Lady Dorothy was involved in so many organisations Jenna would have lost count but for her new improved excellent filing system. Hunt balls, charity concerts, dinners, meetings, it was all a new world for Jenna, one she wouldn't particularly have enjoyed herself, but it was fun to be on the periphery and to have some part in its organisation.

One of the highlights of the September calendar was a big fund-raising dinner for the local lifeboat organisation. The Poultners were away in London and would only arrive back a few hours before the dinner. Every detail had to be checked and covered the previous evening. Jenna was well satisfied with her tasks and was about to retire to her room when Molly and Lois appeared to be having an unseemly row in the kitchen. It appeared the order for a speciality ice-cream di Mascio dessert had gone astray — it should have been received at the factory the day before dinner.

''Tis too late now, they'll be shut,' Molly wailed.

'Send Harry up with it now, he can put the order in the letter box,' Jenna soothed.

'Harry's on silver cleaning and Mr

Took can't spare anyone else.'

'Make something else then, your bomb surprise is brilliant,' Jenna suggested.

'No, Missus was particularly set on this — local you see.' Molly was now in tears.

'Oh, give the order to me,' Jenna said, 'I've still got a key to the factory. I'll put it on Christine's desk marked urgent.'

''Tis a wild night,' Lois said, 'you can't go out in this. Listen to the wind.'

'I've been in worse. I'll enjoy the walk'

'Bless you, Jenna. I'll be waiting up with a hot drink when you're back.'

As she left the house a squall of wind nearly knocked her over, rain splattered her face as she battled towards the cliffs. It was pitch black, the wind a howling banshee and Jenna began to think it was a foolish mission simply for an ice-cream dessert. However the wind eased a little as she turned into the path leading to the factory and as she reached the front door she fumbled in her purse for the order.

'Hey,' a voice yelled out, 'get away from there,' she was caught and held from behind in a rough grasp. 'What are you up . . . Jenna! What on earth . . . ? A flash of lightning illuminated the figure.

'Alessandro . . . what? I thought . . . ?' a crash of thunder deadened her voice as Alessandro unlocked the door and pulled her inside.

'NO,' she struggled.

He switched on the lights, 'Don't be silly, you can't go back out in this storm.'

'I thought you were in Caltarrick.'

'I was but I had to come back here for something. Why did you leave so abruptly? I need you here to help run the business. I'm going back to Italy, so you needn't have gone to the Hall.'

'I . . . I like it there. I've brought an urgent order, it got mislaid — for tomorrow's lifeboat dinner.' She stared at him as though to memorise his features. He was going away! He took her hand as there was a tremendous clap of thunder, a lightning flash and the lights went out. Jenna jumped out in the darkness and found Alessandro's arms. For seconds they held each other in the black dark, then the lights fluttered on and they moved apart.

'I'll take you home, Jenna, I've a van parked on the road.'

'I'm going back to the Hall, I could phone for the car, but I can find my own way.'

Alessandro picked up the phone and held it out to her, 'Dead — we've been having trouble and the storm's knocked out the line again. Come on,' he held out his hand, 'leave the order there, I'll make sure it gets up to the Hall in time.'

The van was parked above the cliff, off the road. Alessandro held her against the buffeting wind and as he opened the van door for her he looked down the cliff. 'There's a light below — it's waving, let's see.'

'No,' she held him back, 'it's nothing,

a trick of the moonlight.'

'There's no moonlight in such a storm. I'm going to look.'

'No, don't.'

In a sudden wind lull a faint cry drifted upwards. 'Help, please help me.'

'Someone's down there.' Alessandro was at the cliff edge peering down.

Faintly the cry came again. 'Help, someone . . . '

Alessandro started to climb over the edge. 'No,' Jenna yelled out, 'come back, you'll fall.'

'No, there's a path, some rocks . . . ' he disappeared for a few seconds then came back up, 'there's someone down there, caught on a ledge.' He shrugged off his coat, 'I'll go down . . . '

'No, let me, I know the path, it's not far down.'

Hand in hand Jenna and Alessandro groped their way down an overgrown path. It was narrow and perilous and the sea raged and boiled beneath them. 'Jenna, go back,' Alessandro begged.

'No, it's all right. Here, the light, it's

over there. Hello,' she yelled, 'someone there?'

'It's me, I'm stuck,' a young voice called.

'Sounds like a boy,' Alessandro said, 'what's a boy doing out here?'

'Shine the light down if you can.' Jenna called to the boy, 'Don't be scared.' The light wavered, swung round and showed up a figure crouching in a small fissure in the rocks.

'I fell down,' the voice quavered, 'from up there. I can't get back. Please, they'll be mad. Hurry.'

'Alessandro, can you get up there?' Jenna pointed to a higher ledge, 'There's an opening in the cliff. Pull the boy in there.'

'I see it.'

Jenna felt, rather than saw, Alessandro climb up the cliff above the boy, he reached down, took the light and then reached for the boy. Jenna pushed from below then hauled herself up and a few seconds later all three were perched on a rocky platform.

She lifted the lantern, a boy's face

shone, scared and frightened. 'Johnny May, what are you doing here?' she asked, knowing full well why he was there.

The boy looked from Jenna to Alessandro and shook his head, 'He'll call the police,' he said, nodding towards Alessandro.

'No he won't, but you should be home in bed, not out here. Let's take you home, you're soaked through, Mr di Mascio has a van parked up there.'

Alessandro reached for the boy who sprang back like a startled rabbit, 'No, you go. Please take him away, Jenna, he'll tell.'

'No he won't. Shush, shush,' she put her arm round the shivering boy and whispered to him softly. As she spoke he looked fearfully behind him then up towards the cliff top. 'There's no-one up there,' she said softly, they'll not be out on a night like this.'

'They are. I've got to wait,' Johnny said, 'please go — with him.'

As Jenna hesitated there was a noise behind them, footsteps and light shining from the blackness, growing brighter. A figure appeared, 'Johnny,' it called out, 'you all right . . . ? Good God, Jenna! What on earth are you doing here . . . and Alessandro, don't you know better than to come prowling round here?' Sam Pascoe glared at his daughter.

'We weren't prowling, I was delivering an order to the factory, Alessandro was there and he offered to drive me home. Then we heard Johnny here cry out, he'd fallen over the cliff. We hauled him back up here.'

'I'll be damned.' Sam Pascoe took off his cap and rubbed his forehead. 'This is a bad business, Jenna.'

'And what are you . . . what are you doing here, Dad? I thought you'd pulled out of all this.'

'I have, but I had to take a message — urgent, lives could have been lost. They're still my mates, Jenna, and I can't let them down.'

'What,' Alessandro stepped forward, 'is going on, Sam?'

Sam looked hard at Jenna, 'Best you don't know. I'll take care of Johnny now, and you two get away from here as fast as you can. The others'll be here soon and one or two of them are not . . . ' He lowered his voice so Johnny couldn't hear as he whispered to Alessandro, 'to be trusted — toss you over that cliff as soon as look at you.

'In fact one or two would love the opportunity I'm 'feared. You're not universally welcome in the village, there's a minority who . . . well they are few — but evil. Just take Jenna back to where she lives now — up at the Hall and forget you ever saw me here, or young Johnny. Talk to him, Jenna, tell him it's serious.'

He held out his hand to the boy, 'Come on, let's move back a bit where 'tis warm and dry. I've a hot drink there too.' He nodded to Alessandro and Jenna and disappeared along a passageway behind the cave, his light bobbing and finally disappearing into the darkness.

The wind was easing and a half moon fitfully parted the clouds for light enough for Jenna and Alessandro to scramble back to the cliff top where the van was parked. He opened the passenger door and Jenna climbed in. 'Well . . . ?' he asked, once in the driver's seat.

'Do you really want to know? The less you know, the safer you will be.'

'I want to know, in fact I can guess. Smuggling isn't it? It does still go on then? Sam's involved in smuggling?'

'He was but since you came and the business took off I thought he'd given it up. I believe him when he said he was the messenger. I only knew about the smuggling a short while ago. Josh Trelawney . . . '

'He's involved?'

'No but some of his older relatives are.'

'I know Cornwall has a reputation for smuggling but I thought that was part history.'

Jenna laughed, 'Mostly it is, but it's in the blood see, it's adventure too,

149

pitting your wits against authority, being an individual, a somebody, and getting a few tax free luxuries as well.'

'What sort? Is it worth it? What if you're caught?'

'Depends who you are. There's quite a network of support, lots in the village have a bit of brandy now and then, French silks, tobacco . . . '

'Aunt Mary?'

'Oh no. Maybe she suspects, but doesn't want to know. Even up at the Hall Lady Dorothy has some fine satin ball gowns, and Lord Poultner's cellar is well stocked with the finest of French wines and cognac. 'Tis common knowledge.'

'Lord Poultner! But he's a magistrate.'

Jenna laughed, 'So he's a good fellow to have on your side.'

For once Alessandro looked at a loss — this was beyond his own culture.

'Don't you have law-breakers in Italy?' Jenna asked, 'isn't there something called the Mafia?'

'Of course you're right, and they can

be a lot more deadly than a few smugglers. I'm sorry but it just doesn't seem to go with a sleepy little Cornish fishing village.'

'Appearances can deceive but you should steer clear of anything to do with smugglers.'

'It's none of my business, I'm well aware I'm an outsider. I just want to build up di Mascio's, maybe some good will come to the county from that.'

They were now at the Hall and rain was still lashing down outside. For a few moments they sat quietly together in the darkness and then, with a sigh, Jenna opened the passenger door. Alessandro held her back, turned her to him, 'You know I want more than just success in di Mascio's, don't you?' He touched her face, kissed her cheek until she felt the tears spring behind her eyes.

'I know, I know, but it's hopeless — we're cousins, so nothing can come of it. Nothing.' She wrenched open the door and turned back to him, 'Keep safe, Alessandro, please keep safe.'

# 9

Later that evening the Poultners returned earlier than expected throwing the household into further turmoil. Lady Dorothy summoned Jenna to her sitting-room, 'I hope all the preparations for the Lifeboat Dinner and Ball are well in hand. I persuaded Lord Alfred to return tonight instead of tomorrow. The Lifeboat Association is one of my favourite charities and I can't afford a thing to go wrong.'

'All in hand, Lady Dorothy. I've checked everything: menu and drinks, with Mr Took of course, the dance band will arrive tomorrow afternoon so there'll be time to tune up and the quartet to play during dinner is already in their accommodation. Transport is arranged to bring them here well before dinner.'

'Excellent, excellent, I see there was

really no need for me to return so early, but I'd had enough of London anyway. Lord Alfred had to be persuaded away from the gaming houses but he came with good grace.'

'I've never been to London,' Jenna said wistfully.

'Not missing a great deal unless of course you enjoy overcrowded streets and noisome smells. Give me Polgrehan air any time. Now, have you a suitable frock to wear?'

'Frock? What for?'

'The Ball, of course. You do have a . . . a ball frock?'

'Why no. I've never needed one — not in Polgrehan.'

'Well, you'll need one for tomorrow evening. That's a pretty enough skirt and blouse you're wearing but hardly suitable for the Lifeboat Dinner and Dance.'

'But am I to be there? I didn't . . . '

'Heavens, child, it's part of your duties. You'll need to check guests against lists — Took will advise on that, you must circulate at the reception, see the guests into dinner, be prepared for any emergency and give Took the nod if any dinner guests . . . er . . . take advantage of our generous wine selection — then make yourself scarce during dinner to check out the ballroom and band.'

'Goodness!' Jenna gasped, 'I'd no idea.'

'What do you think I'm paying you for? You'll do fine, I'm happy with you so far. So, this very important local event will be a challenge.'

'I'm already looking forward to it — except I don't have anything to wear, only my dark grey Sunday suit.'

'Lord above, that'll never do. Go and see Lois, she's got a cupboard full of ball gowns. Best do it tonight in case of alterations.' She narrowed her eyes sizing up Jenna, 'Midnight blue I'd say, maybe azure or forest green, something to set off your lovely hair. Off you go, find Lois.'

Feeling like a favourite dog dismissed to find a new collar, Jenna tracked down Lois in her sitting-room, feet up, cup of tea by her side.

'Quite a day,' Lois sighed, 'what with them coming early. No warning of course, but then we're only servants — nothing else to do but wait hand and foot on M'Lord and Lady.'

Jenna maintained a diplomatic silence until Mrs Lois has grumbled a bit more, then she passed on Lady Dorothy's request. Strangely Mrs Lois perked up at that, got to her feet and took Jenna along to the ground floor bedroom. Here, she flung open wardrobe doors to a cupboard full of ball gowns.

She rummaged through the hangers and pulled out two or three, 'Something here should suit,' she picked out a long dress of dark blue shimmering silk, low cut with figure-clinging waist and hips before flaring out in a layered skirt. 'Try it on,' she stroked the fabric gently, 'and there's shoes to match. Fit you a treat, go on try it.'

Ten minutes later she whipped away the dress, 'it's perfect, just a tuck here and there. I'll do it now. One good turn deserves another, you going out earlier in all that storm.'

'Do you go to the ball?' Jenna asked.

'No fear. It's a night off for me once things get going, of course. Tomorrow will be hectic but once the thing starts you won't see me for dust.'

The day of the Ball was bright and sunny and normally Jenna would have longed to be out in the boat fishing. Usually in late September or even into October there was only a trickle of visitors, leaving the village quiet and peaceful, but Poultner Hall was anything but peaceful as preparations were under way for the event of the year. Caterers rushed in and out, Mr Took was everywhere organising and supervising, florist carts brought huge bouquets and tubs of greenery.

Jenna's heart missed a beat as she saw the di Mascio ice cart deliver the famous dessert but she didn't know the driver and had little time to think of Alessandro. Later in the day guests arrived in cars and taxis from the station. Most would be staying over the weekend for the hunting and fishing.

Finally, an hour before the reception all went quiet as guests bathed and changed. Jenna had about ten minutes to change after checking last minute details and only seconds to register the stranger in the long mirror elegantly dressed in a flattering ball gown, dark curls caught up away from her face. Lady Dorothy had loaned her a gold necklace at the last minute which glistened on her smooth skin.

'Whee,' Jenna said to the mirror, 'that can't be me.' She scuttled downstairs to her place in the reception hall, discreetly shadowing Mr Took as he announced the dinner guests.

She knew very few of the guests, they were mainly gentlemen and ladies of the Country set, some from London, one or two familiar names announced with great authority by Mr Took.

Just before dinner was served Jenna's stomach dropped. 'Senor Alessandro di

Mascio with Miss Christine Polglaze.'

She looked towards the entrance, saw Alessandro looking impossibly attractive in evening dress, Christine clinging to his arm in an startling red dress and white feather boa. She turned away but not before she'd met Alessandro's eyes, barely smiling as he greeted Lord and Lady Poultner.

She turned away as the guests began to file into the dining-room, desperately wondering how she could escape the rest of the evening.

It seemed to go on for ever, dinner took an age, there were lots of speeches, the quartet played between courses, but finally dinner ended and the ball began as dancing got under way and now the lesser status guests streamed in, local lifeboat men and their wives who were always invited to the Ball. Soon the ballroom was packed.

Jenna, of course, was still on duty, but Lady Dorothy had encouraged her to mingle, making sure everyone had a good time. She kept an eye open for lonely wallflowers and sent any available male to dance with them.

'Jenna Pascoe! What a sight for sore eyes. Where'd you get that gown? What a get-up.'

'Josh! Of course, you're lifeboat crew, aren't you?'

'Yes, and my brother and uncles are here. It's a grand do, isn't it? Can you dance with me?'

'I suppose so, it's my job to mix and mingle.'

'Fine.' He took her in his arms and moved on to the floor. 'Enjoying your new job?'

'Yes, I am, it's . . . very varied.' They danced for a while, she'd always enjoyed dancing with Josh and in earlier years they'd gone to village dances together. Now as he steered her expertly round the floor he looked worried. 'What's up, Josh?' Jenna said, 'you're not concentrating.'

'No.' Abruptly he led her away from the main body of dancers into an empty side room.

'What's the matter? Aren't you enjoying the dance?'

'Jen, I could dance with you all night, you know that.'

'I'm sorry, but . . . '

'It's all right, Jen, I know where I stand but I'm real fond of you. I don't want anything to happen to . . . '

'What? What are you talking about?'

'Just tell me — you're not working at the factory any more?'

'Course not. I'm pretty busy here.'

'I can see that . . . so, you wouldn't be working there . . . up at Polglaze at all?'

'No, I've said. What are you on about?'

'I can't say any more but there's trouble brewing and I don't want you involved.'

'What sort of trouble? You must tell me.'

'I can't, it's more than my life's worth. Just keep away from the factory, that's all.'

'You've got to tell me . . . '

'No, I can't. Most likely nothing will happen — there's a lot of talk going on without any action. Just be careful, Jenna. Now let's get back to the dance because I'm not saying another word.'

In fact she didn't see Josh again until the National Anthem brought the festivities to a conclusion. After the dance with Josh, Jenna had found herself much in demand as a dance partner — even Lord Poultner insisted on twirling her round a polka until he was so red in the face she was alarmed for his health.

As the crowd began to thin Alessandro sought her out, 'Jenna, you look beautiful. I should have liked to dance with you but . . . '

'Best not — really. You've enjoyed the evening?'

'I came to say goodbye. I'm going to Florence tomorrow. My mother and Rob will run the business while I'm away . . . and Christine, of course.'

'Aren't you coming back?' Jenna was fearful.

'I have work to do in Florence and in Santini too in case Mamma wants to return there. At present she is moving back to Harbour View with Francesca now the season is over. Now we have to consolidate what we have achieved here,' he spoke automatically, his eyes never leaving Jenna's face.

'I . . . I shall miss you.'

'I know that but . . . '

'Oh hello, Jenna,' Christine came towards them, 'what a splendid party. Aren't I lucky, I'd never have been invited but for Alessandro.'

'I'm glad you enjoyed it.'

'I did, I did. We'll get together soon, Jen, call at the farm sometime.'

'Yes I will.' Jenna smiled but her heart was breaking as she watched Christine take Alessandro's arm as they went to take their leave of Lord and Lady Poultner. At the door Alessandro turned and smiled at Jenna, a smile that crushed her heart even more.

The Lifeboat Ball marked the end of Lady Dorothy's really hectic season and

Jenna was not so busy, she'd organised the routine so efficiently she had more free time for herself, time to worry about Josh Trelawney's warning.

She went home more frequently to spend time with her mother and aunt. Visitors were still booking in at Harbour View, but Mary Pascoe was coping well and now loved having Olivia and Francesca to live there too.

The ice-cream parlour at Caltarrick was closed for renovation and extension with Olive spending time at the Polglaze factory where new equipment was being installed. The ice-cream vans and carts still worked the lanes and took stands at autumn fairs so the factory kept fairly busy. Jenna worried whenever her aunt worked late there but as the days went by she began to forget about Josh's warning, putting it down to an over-dramatic nature. Josh always had made a drama out of any crisis.

Then, just as she began to settle into a steady routine between work and at the Hall and Harbour View, a couple of incidents occurred which caused her fears to resurface. On her day off she went to Harbour View for supper, she'd taken Clarrie and Francesca for a walk along the cliffs and then blackberrying in the fields behind. Coming home with full baskets she'd found Rob in an agitated state of fury.

'Ran me down deliberately he did,' Jenna heard as she went into the house. 'Deserted road, plenty of room, came straight at me, cart overturned just like Joe Edwards, only this time it was a motor that drove at me.'

'You're sure you were on the right side of the road,' Mary asked anxiously.

'Course I was. Neddy's a steady old horse, plods along right on course. Time I had a van though — they'd balk at running into one of our vans.'

'Could it have been an accident?' Jenna said.

'Could have, but wasn't, mark my words.'

Mary was worried, 'do you think we

164

should let Alessandro know?'

Olivia shook her head, 'No, there's nothing he could do about it and he's really busy now. We have to assume it was an accident.'

But the next incident was no accident and it was a policeman from Caltarrick who brought the news that the ice-cream parlour there had been damaged, windows broken, tables and chairs smashed, equipment broken. Both Rob and Matt went with Olivia to inspect the damage and reported a sorry state to Mary and Jenna.

'Pounds worth of damage, it'll need completely redecorating. Fortunately the equipment can be repaired and it's a blessing the new stuff hadn't arrived.'

'It's serious, Aunt Olivia, you just see what we have to let Alessandro know.'

'No, not yet. Let's wait and see what'll happen next, we're being targeted, someone's out to ruin the di Mascio business.'

Matt agreed, 'We can't let that happen. Jenna, what do you think?'

'I really don't know. I'm not part of it any more . . . '

'But you were, and you're family. We have to stand together. Who could possibly want to ruin us?'

Jenna frowned. 'I don't know,' Josh Trelawney's warning rung through her head, 'perhaps we ought at least to let Alessandro know what's happening.'

'No,' Olivia spoke firmly, 'I'll talk to the police, see if they have any ideas.'

Just then Sam Pascoe came into the room, he looked angry and worried. 'Sam,' Mary went to him, 'what do you think we should do?'

'Do about what?' He hung his jacket on the back door, 'I hope you've left me some supper. Hello Jenna, nice to see you home. How's life in the upper strata?'

'It's not like that, Dad. Quite homely actually.'

Sam snorted, 'Oh aye: two footmen, a butler, brigade of servants, a fleet of gardeners . . . '

'Dad!' Matt put in, 'Jenna says the

Poultners are decent folk — and I know they are.'

'I'll tell you something, there's talk of a war, a big European conflict. Bloke in Germany, Adolf Hitler, looking for trouble. Once we're at war we can forget about the ice-cream parlours and factories, you'll all be fighting for your lives and . . . '

'Stop it, Sam,' Mary cried, 'we've enough bother without you adding to it with talk about war.'

'Let's have some supper then if you haven't eaten the lot.' He sat down with a scowl. It was unlike Sam to be so belligerent and it was obvious to Jenna that something serious was bothering him.

Olivia organised repairs for the parlour at Caltarrick, installed more security on the premises and the police promised to keep an eye on things. The inspector had decided vandals from outside the area were to blame and that it was a one off occurrence, not to be repeated. But there was tension in the air, a tension which spread to Polgrehan.

War rumours started to filter from London, the future looked uncertain. At Poultner Hall Lord Alfred began to talk about staff cuts, there were mysterious meetings late at night in Lord Alfred's study. At one of these meetings housekeeper, Lois, asked Jenna to take in whisky and sandwiches as talk looked likely to go on into the small hours.

Jenna paused at the heavy door, put the large tray on a side table, raised her hand to knock and held back as she heard, 'Polglaze Farm, a diversion — kill two birds with one stone.'

Then Lord Alfred's voice, 'I can't countenance that, no-one must be hurt . . . '

'Just to divert . . . '

Then abruptly the door was flung open and Lord Alfred stood in the doorway. 'Jenna!'

'I've brought the whisky and sand-wiches you sent for.' She picked up the tray.

Lord Alfred stopped her, 'I'll take them in — in a moment.' He closed the door behind him, stepped away taking Jenna's arm, 'Tell me, Jenna, this, er factory at George Polglaze's farm, is it occupied much now the season's over?'

'I don't know, I don't work there now.'

'I know that, but your brothers do and your aunt. Olive Kittow as was.'

'Yes but she's mainly at Caltarrick except . . .'

'No night shifts now?'

'Not that I know of.'

'Alessandro, the boss of the outfit, where's he?'

'In Florence I believe.'

'Righto,' he patted her shoulder, 'you're a good girl, Lady Dorothy says you're invaluable. Just hold the door will you while I take the tray.' He winked at her, 'Thirsty work these meetings.'

Jenna held the door open while he carried through the heavy tray. She tried to see the men inside but they mainly had their backs to her. At one end of the table she recognised Jim Penhallorick, next to him Vincent Trelawney, an uncle of Josh's, and a couple of younger men who were vaguely familiar but not of the village.

The door closed, she put her ear to it, there was a general hubbub as the sandwiches were sent round then Penhallorick's voice, 'Agreed then, next moonless night. We'll check winds and tides. Lord Alfred you'll do your bit?'

'Of course. The usual for the Chief Constable?'

A murmur of agreement then Jenna heard clearly, 'But no-one's to be hurt, mind.' It was Lord Alfred speaking but this time the murmur of agreement was more muted.

Someone suddenly said, 'That girl isn't listening by the door by any chance?' Footsteps crossed the room and Jenna fled.

All night Jenna tossed and turned unable to sleep, pondering the significance of what she'd heard, and could only conclude that there was some threat to the ice-cream factory, possibly driven by Jim Penhallorick to damage the di Mascio ice-cream business. But why would Lord Alfred be involved in such a scheme? He was a magistrate, a man of standing in the county. What possible interest could he possibly have in ruining a good business that was benefiting his county?

She wondered if she should confide in Lady Dorothy but dismissed the idea immediately. As dawn broke she suddenly thought of a connection involving Lord Alfred and it didn't reassure her one little bit as to the safety of the Polglaze factory. Even if she was right there was nothing she could do except watch and wait.

She thought about talking to her father or Rob but they would scoff and call her an alarmist. Perhaps Alessandro would know what to do but how could she reach him in faraway Florence. She could only wait and be vigilant.

As the days passed without incident

Jenna began to think she had imagined the significance of the conversation behind closed doors. She relaxed and turned her attention to Lady Dorothy's social calendar, events now building up to the Christmas season even though October was only midway. The early autumn days were fine and warm, the sea calm and gentle.

She thought frequently of Alessandro and wondered what he was doing in Florence. Olivia had reported the Santini reconstruction was going well, she still couldn't decide whether to return to her Italian life. Polgrehan was daily exerting a stronger grip on her and her sister, Mary, prayed she would remain.

One evening Lord Alfred announced he was going to London for a few days, some unexpected business needed his attention and no, he didn't want Lady Dorothy to come with him on this occasion.

'This has left me in a pickle,' she frowned at Jenna, 'we've several local arrangements where we both should be attending. I don't know what he's thinking about. However, we must make the best of it and reschedule the days.' She handed Jenna a list. Can you work late tonight, finish off these letters so they can go first post tomorrow. I know it's late but . . .'

'It's no problem, Lady Dorothy, I can stay here overnight to finish if I need to.'

'Good girl. Take time off in lieu later in the week.' She gave Jenna a sharp look, 'you're looking a bit peaky my dear, everything all right?'

'Yes, it's er . . . I'm often a bit low in spirits as the dark nights begin,' she lied.

'Hmph. A long way to go until next spring. Don't overdo it, I'll be back later this evening.'

Jenna started on the pile of correspondence, the Lifeboat Association needed to check its dates for next year's Ball. She fetched the calendar and drew a quick breath. Tonight there would be no moon! She glanced out of the window — it was pitch black and overcast. She felt a tremor of alarm, dismissed it as foolish, checked the calendar and as a precaution reached for the telephone to check Harbour View. Lady Dorothy had given her permission to use it as she wished. She gave the operator the number — it rang for ages before Mary answered.

'Hello,' tentative, uncertain, her mother hated the telephone but it was a guest house necessity.

'Mum, it's me.'

'Oh Jenna, thank goodness.'

'Why, what's wrong?'

'Nothing . . . I just . . . you know how I am about telephones. Is there anything the matter?' To Mary, telephones, like telegrams, were associated with bad news rather than good business.

'No, just a call to see if everyone's all right.'

'Why wouldn't they be. Is this call costing money for Lady Poultner?'

'Oh Mother, don't fuss. Where is everybody?' She tried to sound casual but she could almost see her mother's frown.

'I don't know. Rob went to The Pilchards with Matt and Dad. I'm just here with Clarrie.'

'Aunt Olivia?'

'She's gone to Polglaze Farm, some stuff about accounts to sort out. She took Francesca who couldn't sleep for some reason. She should be back soon.'

'She's at the factory?'

'Yes dear but . . . '

'I must go, Mum. I'll speak to you later.'

'Yes, but . . . '

Jenna put the phone down with a terrible feeling that tonight, moonless and black, would see more disaster for the di Mascios. She pushed Lady Dorothy's papers back into the file and picked up the phone, 'Please, Aunt Olivia, answer the phone.' She could hear it ringing then abruptly the line went dead. She tried again — still dead.

She tried the operator, 'Please, you must try, it's urgent.'

'No, there must be a fault. I'll report . . . '

But Jenna was already running to fetch her coat and was out of the front door of Poultner Hall in seconds. Aunt Olivia and Francesca were alone at Polglaze Farm. For a moment she hesitated, she could telephone the farm, their line would surely be working, and warn the Polglazes — then she remembered that all three Polglazes were away, George Polglaze's brother had died up country and the family had left for the Midlands that morning.

The grandfather clock showed 8.45 as she left the Hall. It would take her at least half-an-hour to reach Polglaze unless she took a shortcut through the woods.

# 10

Jenna moved through the dark woods by pure instinct praying she was going in the right direction. She recalled that the track went downhill toward the shore then looped left uphill toward the cliff top, coming out by the road near Polglaze Farm. Arms outstretched she felt her way through the trees stumbling once or twice over twisted roots. Trees gave way to undergrowth so she reckoned she was near the road. Suddenly a couple of birds flew upwards with squawking shrieks and Jenna stopped as she saw a glimmer of light in the woods behind her.

A voice called out sharply, 'Hey, who's there?'

Jenna froze, hardly breathing.

Again the voice called, 'Come out of there.'

Another voice answered, ''Tis only

night birds, you damn fool. Shut up and keep quiet.'

Jenna knew now that if her aunt was still in the factory she and Francesca would be in danger — the men in the woods were not out for a nocturnal stroll. She waited until the light had disappeared then cautiously made her way up to the road. Once there she could see the back of the farm buildings. Softly and silently she ran up the road and crossed into the Polglaze fields. A couple of horses, used to pull the di Mascio carts, were in the fields and neighed softly as they sensed Jenna's approach.

'Hush, hush,' she whispered. Now she was through the gate next to the factory building. At first she thought it was in darkness and breathed a sigh of relief until she saw the light from the office window. Aunt Olivia must still be in there and the men in the woods would be close by.

She broke into a run and reached the heavy front door which was unlocked.

She called out, 'Aunt Olivia, it's Jenna. Quickly, you've got to leave.'

'Whatever's the matter?' Olivia turned from her desk, 'why are you here at this time of night?'

'I'll explain later, just get out of here. Where's Francesca? Is your van nearby?'

'Yes. Just round the side . . . '

'Quick, get Francesca and run to the van. I'll explain once we're on the road.'

Olivia picked up the sleeping child from a makeshift bed on the floor, 'She hasn't been sleeping lately . . . '

'Never mind now, just hurry.'

'I must lock up.' She went to the front door.

'No, there's no time. Where's the van?'

'There, just by the door.' She peered out into the darkness. 'Oh Jenna, it's gone. Where . . . ?'

'Get back inside the building. Lock the door.' Jenna bundled her aunt back into the building, slammed the door and shot the bolts.

'Jenna, you must explain why . . . '

She was interrupted by a rattle as

stones were flung at the windows.

'Upstairs,' Jenna pulled her aunt to the foot of the stairs leading to a storage room which was piled high with cartons and bags of sugar. Francesca woke and started to whimper.

'Hush, go back to sleep,' Olivia soothed but now the commotion below was loud and raucous. Stones were flung at all the windows, there was tremendous banging on the main door as though a battering ram was being used. 'Whatever's going on?'

'Someone's out to sabotage the factory. I suspected it but didn't know it would be like this.'

'Well I'm not stopping in here like a cornered rat, I'm going to put a stop to it. You take Francesca . . . '

'No, it's too dangerous, come away.'

But Olivia opened the front door and yelled out, 'Just stop all this. Go away before I call the police.'

'That's her,' a drunken voice yelled out, 'we don't want the likes of you back here.'

A stone was flung at Olivia, followed by another. The yelling increased and Jenna realised they were at the mercy of a drunken mob. She pulled her aunt back in and slammed the door. Almost immediately the battering started up again and to Jenna's horror, fire glowed through the windows.

'My God, they're setting the place on fire, we can't stay here. I tried to phone you . . .'

'It's dead. I tried earlier to phone Mary.'

'We must get out of here,' Jenna looked around the factory in desperation.

'Is there a back way out,' Olivia asked, now anxious for their safety as the yelling of the men continued.

'I don't think so . . . wait, there must be another way out.'

'Of course, through the office . . . there's a door at the back but it's always locked — there isn't a key.'

A large stone crashed through the window shattering glass, leaving a gaping hole. Dark jeering faces were framed in the broken window. 'Come out you Jezebel.' A huge man practically filled the frame. 'Give us a torch from the fire — we'll smoke them out,' he bellowed.

Olivia, enraged, picked up an axe from a rack and swung at the man who momentarily backed off in alarm. 'Jenna, that door, take that bigger axe, smash it through. We can't stay here.'

Francesca was now wailing in terror, increasing in volume as a flaming piece of wood was hurled through the window. Jenna put Francesca down, picked up the axe and smote the door with it. Nothing happened, she tried again and this time the timbers cracked. 'Nearly there,' she yelled. At the next blow the door yielded, she could see through to the road behind. 'Quick, Auntie, through here, they can't see us.' She picked up Francesca who clung to her fearfully. 'It's all right, Fran, just a few silly men.'

'Uncle Aless, Uncle Aless,' the child whimpered.

Jenna added her own prayer for a miracle as she saw the room behind smoke-filled, her aunt gasping for breath.

'I can't . . . you take Fran.'

Jenna held her breath and went to Olivia. 'Come on, just across the room, the door's down, just a few steps.'

'No, there are men round the back, lots more. Oh Jenna, I'm so sorry . . . '

'We must try.'

By now the noise outside was deafening and there were other sounds too, motor vehicles, horns blaring. Olivia sank to the floor coughing, clutching her throat but Jenna took her arm and with all her strength dragged her across the floor towards the hole in the door. Cool air blew in.

Olivia caught her breath and stood up. 'There are too many of them, it's hopeless.' She took Francesca from Jenna and clutched her to her chest, 'Shush, shush . . . '

'They won't hurt a child,' Jenna said.

'They're out for blood,' Olivia gasped, 'we're in for it.'

'Uncle Aless, Uncle . . . ' Francesca strained away from her granny.

'No pet, no, he's . . . my God — Alessandro!'

'Stand away from the door, Mamma.' He swung a great hammer and the wood shattered. 'Mamma, Francesca, you're all right now, the police are here, fire brigade on its way. Come through here, my car's right by the door.'

'Get Jenna,' Olivia coughed.

'Jenna's here?'

'She came to warn me. Where is she?'

'Here.' Jenna came through the smoke, flames now flanned by the fresh air from the open door. 'Alessandro!' she blinked as he took her in his arms.

'My God, Jenna, if I'd have known . . . ' he clasped her to him and kissed her.

She gave a sigh and yielded to his kiss.

Olivia watched them with a look of utter desperation on her face.

For seconds they remained a frozen tableau until shouts from outside drew them out of the factory and into the open where powerful torches illuminated the scene.

'Jenna!' it was Rob followed by Matt and Sam, 'Are you all right? What the hell were you doing here? Thank God you're safe.'

'What . . . what happened?' Jenna blinked at the number of men surrounding the factory.

'Let's get you all home first,' Sam said, 'you ma's sick with worry. We'll leave the police to round up these villains who tried to burn the place down.'

'But why?' Olivia was in tears, holding on to Alessandro.

'They're not from Polgrehan,' Alessandro said, 'hired thugs from town. Let's take you home now. You're safe, I'm so sorry you and Francesca were here, Mamma, I never thought . . . until Aunt Mary told us.' He nodded to Sam and Rob, 'Well done. I'll take them back to Harbour View now.'

'We'll follow,' Sam said. 'I can hear

the fire brigade, fire's already dying down. It's all over.'

Later at Harbour View after a sleepy Francesca had been soothed, comforted and put to bed, Olivia and Jenna were told what had happened. 'Polglaze factory wasn't the real target,' Sam said, 'it was meant to be a diversion to keep the police occupied. Of course it was Jim Penhallorick's idea though I don't suppose for a moment he realised what could happen — he thought 'two birds with one stone'; damage his business rival, Alessandro, by damaging his factory, thus providing cover for one of the biggest smuggling operations ever. Penhallorick was in the cave waiting for the boats when Polglaze was attacked.'

'Smuggling?' Mary looked horrified, 'You're never involved in that, Sam Pascoe?'

'Not now love, though I have been and I'm not ashamed of it. It was fair game in the past but recently out-of-county criminal elements have highjacked it. Even Jim Penhallorick's scared of them. This run was supposed to be the last.'

'But, Lord Alfred, surely he's not part of it,' Jenna said.

'Yes, he has been, but even he's taken fright, pushed off to London to be out of the way in case anything went wrong, which it did. The attack on the factory got out of hand, and once they realised women were trapped inside . . . ' Sam shuddered, 'If ever I get the chance to get my hands on them . . . ' He took a reassuring pull at his cider.

'But how did you know when the attack and the smuggling were going to happen,' Olivia asked.

'I heard rumours in the village,' Rob answered, 'and out on my rounds with the ice-cream cart. Everyone was scared, but Josh Trelawney told me — he was worried about his uncles, one of them was being blackmailed by the gang. Vincent Trelawney was in deep and Josh wanted it all to end, and fortunately Alessandro turned up just in time.

And end it did. The gang who attacked the factory were all in jail awaiting trial as were the smugglers apprehended by the Customs Officers. Jim Penhallorick and the Trelawneys who weren't involved at sea got away with it but they'd had a real scare. After centuries major smuggling between Brittany and Polgrehan was over for good.

The whole village was chastened by the affair and when it was known that little Francesca had been in danger Polgrehan presented a solid wall of support for Olivia and her family. Prayers and thanks to God were said in chapel and a village delegation sought out Alessandro thanking him for stimulating the local economy and promising every support. Jim Penhallorick wisely decided to retire from the ice-cream business as well as from smuggling. He offered his Polgrehan business to Alessandro at a fair price.

A week after the Polglaze attack a family conference was once again convened at Harbour View. Jenna was given the day off to say farewell to cousin, Alessandro.

'Such a pity he's decided to go back to Italy,' Lady Dorothy said, 'we could do with more like him to get our economy moving.'

'My brothers, Rob and Matt, are taking over and I'm sure they'll do well,' Jenna said distractedly, wishing the day was over and that Alessandro had gone and she could start to try and put him from her heart.

'I'm sure they will but they don't quite have the . . . the glamour of Alessandro di Mascio do they? Good lads both of course,' she added quickly. 'Enjoy your day, Jenna. See you tomorrow.'

Mary and Olivia had put on one of their special dinners. There were only a couple of guests in the house and they were out for the day. When they left Mary and Sam would close Harbour View for extensive repairs and renovations, mainly at Olivia's suggestion.

Mary was fired up again with enthusiasm for the project and now both Rob and Matt brought in good money from the di Mascio business, life was so much easier for her.

Mary and Jenna served up a roast dinner. Jenna couldn't eat at all and Alessandro picked at his, glancing at Jenna so many times Olivia began to look in increasing anguish from one to the other.

'Mamma,' Alessandro said, 'you still haven't told me your decision. I must leave soon and I should like to know your future plans.'

'Yes, I'm sorry, I should have told you before but it's been a difficult decision. I'm not coming back with you now, you knew that of course, but I'm still not sure. I am torn, and now the people of Polgrehan have accepted me . . .'

'Mamma, there is no hurry, Santini is nowhere near finished. I should be happy to have you remain here. You could keep an eye on Rob and Matt . . .'

'Yes, do please,' both lads spoke at once, 'we'd both be happier if you were here — all your experience . . . '

Olivia laughed. 'Well that will be a challenge. All right, I'll stay until further notice. How's that?'

'Excellent.' Sam and Mary nodded agreement.

'Good, that's settled.' Alessandro stood up. 'So, I can go now. I am truly sorry to leave,' he kissed his mother and aunt, shook hands with the men folk and hugged Clarrie and Francesca. 'Where's Jenna?'

'Outside I think, in the garden. Shall I call her in?'

'No, no. I'll say goodbye to her. Please, all of you, finish your meal. I hate goodbyes.' He went swiftly out of the house.

Jenna was standing by his car, her eyes misted with tears. 'Alessandro, I can't bear this. It seems so . . . so wrong.'

'I know. Give me a few minutes, walk down to the beach with me, away from the house . . . '

'They can see us from where they are.'

'They're not looking. Please, just five minutes.' He took her hand and together they walked the short way to the beach, deserted now, a strong autumnal wind whipping up the incoming tide. He took her in his arms, 'I don't want to leave you, you know that. I love you, Jenna, you know that too, I don't care if we are cousins I can't live without you. Come with me — please.'

He bent to kiss her, held her so fiercely she cried out, 'Alessandro, don't. You're breaking my heart. Go, please now . . . ' She tore herself from his embrace and turned away from him, looking out to sea.

He lifted his arms in a gesture of despair, dropped them to his sides and walked slowly back towards his car.

Jenna ran towards the sea, stumbled over a large rock and collapsed on to it, covered her face sobbing desperately.

Olivia, going upstairs to check on Francesca witnessed the scene from the bedroom window. She gasped as in pain and clutched her heart in agony. 'No, no, please, not that. It can't happen, it mustn't!'

She stayed riveted to the window as Alessandro came back to Harbour View to take his bags from the front door to his car. He looked away from the beach deliberately and Olivia called out soundlessly as the tide rushed towards the rocks where Jenna was sitting, head bent in despair.

'Aless . . . ' Olivia dashed down the stairs across the road and on to the beach. 'Jenna, come away. The tide . . .'

'Oh Aunt Olivia, I can't stand it. I know it's wrong but I love him. I love my cousin, Alessandro, I'm so sorry . . . and now he's gone.'

Olivia clasped her hands in prayer and closed her eyes. 'Forgive me, forgive me,' she silently mouthed, then threw her head back and pulled Jenna from the rock.'

Rob came running down the beach, 'What's going on, Auntie? Why's Jenna trying to drown herself?'

'She's not. Now you run quickly, Alessandro's in his car. STOP HIM going, tell him, tell him his . . . tell him I say he MUST come back. Go, go.' She gave him a quick push.

'Rightio,' Rob sped up the beach as Alessandro was fiddling with the starting handle.

Olivia turned back to Jenna, 'Jenna come into the house, you're soaked . . . '

'I don't want . . . I can't . . . '

'Yes you can . . . you've done nothing wrong. You see . . . ' she sighed, 'Alessandro di Mascio is not your cousin.'

Olivia di Mascio sat close to her sister Mary, and as she forced out her sad tale frequently reached out to clutch her before continuing. Alessandro and Jenna sat side by side, close but not quite touching, barely able to believe what Olivia was telling them. Rob and Matt had volunteered to take the little girls out to play — they would hear the story later.

Olivia found it hard to begin, she

looked pleadingly at Alessandro. 'Mamma he said gently, tell us please, you have to . . . '

'I know, but I've lived so long with . . . the past buried . . . it's hard to recall.'

'Take your time,' Sam said.

She drew a long breath. 'When I was a young girl I had a friend from schooldays, Elizabeth Kelly, Betty we called her. We grew up together.'

'I remember Betty,' Mary broke in, 'a beautiful girl, so pretty, lively.'

'Exactly. Betty and I were good friends but we were a bad influence on each other, we had wild streaks. We egged each other on, were often in trouble . . . '

'I don't remember . . . ' Mary frowned.

'Ssh, Mum,' Jenna put her fingers to her lips.

'As you know I was engaged to Bert Trelawney, that is until Angelo, my husband to be, appeared with the Strolling Players at Polgrehan Fish Festival. Wonderful performance they

195

gave. Angelo and Mario . . . '

'Mario?' Alessandro queried.

Olivia hung her head. 'Betty fell in love with Mario, just as I did with Angelo. We were both headstrong, passionate, selfish,' she lifted her head, 'and we both became pregnant — to the shame and horror of our respective parents. I at least was given a choice — to go into a home for unmarried mothers, have the baby there, then give it up for adoption. If I refused to do that, I was to be disowned, never to come to Polgrehan again, I was to be banished from the home I loved, erased from the family memory. I chose Angelo and my baby.'

'Terrible,' Jenna murmured. Alessandro took her hand.

'That's how it was then,' said Sam, 'and still is too in many cases.'

'And Betty?' Jenna asked.

'She had no choice. Her father, a strict Methodist, was a councillor, he had some influence nationally and immediately had Mario deported and Betty imprisoned in one of those homes for 'fallen girls', and he chose the worst one he could find.' Her voice shook, 'I . . . I'm sorry.'

'I'll make some tea,' Sam said.

Olivia put her hand out to stop him, 'No, let me finish. Angelo and I went to London, married and went to Italy where I was warmly welcomed by his family. His mother looked after me as her own daughter. I loved her and Angelo's family too. We were happy, excited about the baby when we heard the dreadful news . . . ' Now tears would not be held back, Olivia sobbed and sobbed until Alessandro went to sit by her and held her hand.

'Mamma, go on.'

She gave a shuddering sigh, 'Mario, desperate to get Betty back, jumped ship on the way back from Italy . . . and was drowned.'

'Oh no,' Jenna cried out, 'how dreadful. Poor Betty.'

'Indeed, and the awful thing was her parents took pleasure in telling her the news. She smuggled out a letter to me saying her father was going to put the baby in a children's' home, not for adoption, but as slave labour eventually. Betty was desperate, we appealed to the di Mascio family who gave us money to come back to England, we were determined to rescue Betty from that dreadful place . . . '

She stopped, took a breath and said quickly, 'How we got her out is another story, but we managed and planned to take her back to Italy with us. She was well into her pregnancy, I was several weeks behind. In London, before we could cross to Italy, Betty went into labour. We took her to hospital . . . it was a long hard birth and Betty, my lovely, lively girl simply gave up.

'I believe she gave up because she wanted to be with Mario. She lived just long enough to have his baby . . . and,' now she turned and looked directly at Alessandro, 'forgive me, but you were that baby. You are the son of Betty Kelly and Mario Bonelli.' The silence was only broken by the steady tick of the mantle clock.

Finally Alessandro said, 'Mario Bonelli? Then I'm not a di Mascio?'

'Yes you are. We adopted you as soon as we possibly could and you took Angelo's family name. Mario was distantly related to the di Mascios from his mother's side.'

'So,' he took a deep breath and the look he gave Jenna was one of pure joy, 'so we are not cousins. Thank God — I knew it, I felt it in my bones. Thank you, Mamma, thank you . . .'

'But I am not your ma . . .'

He leapt up, lifted Olivia off her feet and hugged her until she gasped for breath, 'You are, of course you are, you are the dearest Mamma a son could have, as was Angelo my dearest father.'

'And what happened to your . . . your baby?' Jenna asked as Alessandro released Olivia and put his arm round Jenna herself.

'That was my great sadness, whether it was the stress, or the travelling, or some would say punishment for the trouble I had caused, my sin could not be condoned. I went into premature labour the day before we were due to leave England, my . . . ' she stopped to wipe away the tears from her face, 'my son was born, a tiny scrap of a boy, far too tiny to survive.

'He died at the hospital, we took his little body to Italy where he is buried in a private place. Angelo and I used to make a pilgrimage every year to grieve, and to thank God for giving us Alessandro to care for.'

'And you did care for me and loved me. I will always be your son, Mamma, and give thanks for what you did. Why have you kept this terrible secret to yourself?'

'When we brought you back to Italy the di Mascio's swore to take you as their own and you would in fact become a di Mascio — and to them that meant no-one should know the truth. It was to be kept a solemn family secret — Angelo and I had to swear an oath before God,' she crossed herself.

'I had to break that oath because I finally saw the unhappiness you and Jenna were suffering. I hope I will be forgiven but I couldn't hurt my own family again — after what I'd done to my sister.'

'I reckon you've made up for that a thousand times over,' Sam said, 'and we need something stronger than tea to celebrate this turn up for the books. I'll just nip out to The Pilchards . . . er . . . Jenna, Alessandro, is it true, I never noticed aught between you.'

'I loved Jenna right away,' Alessandro said swiftly, 'but knew, as cousins, we couldn't marry so we tried to fight it. That's why Jenna went to Poultner Hall and I returned unhappily to Italy — but I couldn't stay away, I had to come back even though I knew . . . '

'Ssh,' Jenna put her fingers to his lips, 'don't . . . that's over now and we can be happy together. Thank you Aunt Olivia.' She kissed her aunt and turned back to Alessandro.

Alessandro took her hand in his and faced Sam and Mary, 'Sam and Mary, Aunt and Uncle, have I your permission to ask Jenna, your daughter, to marry me?'

'Go ahead, lad if she's willing. Eh Mary?' Sam had a broad grin on his face and a tear in his eye.

'Jenna Pascoe,' Alessandro looked deeply into her shining eyes, I declare my love for you before your families. I love you, I want to marry you, I want to share our lives and never be apart. Please, Jenna?'

'Yes, yes. Yes, Alessandro di Mascio, I love you too and cannot think of life without you, Italy or Cornwall, wherever you go I go with you.'

They kissed to bind the solemn promise just as Rob and Matt returned with the girls to hear the whole sad story once more, except this time the story had a happy ending with the joyous union of Alessandro and Jenna.

SUSPICIOUS HEART
EDEN IN PARADISE
SWEET CHALLENGE
FOREVER IN MY HEART

We do hope that you have enjoyed reading this large print book.

Did you know that all of our titles are available for purchase?

We publish a wide range of high quality large print books including:
**Romances, Mysteries, Classics General Fiction Non Fiction and Westerns**

Special interest titles available in large print are:
**The Little Oxford Dictionary Music Book, Song Book Hymn Book, Service Book**

Also available from us courtesy of Oxford University Press:
**Young Readers' Dictionary (large print edition) Young Readers' Thesaurus (large print edition)**

For further information or a free brochure, please contact us at:
**Ulverscroft Large Print Books Ltd., The Green, Bradgate Road, Anstey, Leicester, LE7 7FU, England.
Tel:** (00 44) **0116 236 4325
Fax:** (00 44) **0116 234 0205**

# NEVER LOOK BACK

## Janet Roscoe

Nina, anxious to save her marriage to Charles, wants to stop the rot before it's too late. Charles, refusing to admit that there is anything wrong, tells Nina to stop imagining problems. But there is her step-brother, Duncan Stevens — easy-going and artistic, everything that Charles is not . . . Charles' sister-in-law likens divorce to a mere game of chess — yet the effect of a tragic death, seven years previously, triggers off a happening of such magnitude that Nina faces the truth at last.

# PASSPORT TO FEAR

## Patricia Hutchinson

Rose and Ray, two young women travelling by ship from India to England are alike in appearance. Both orphans, Ray is wealthy, while Rose has lived on her wits. Ray has a heart condition and is going to England to her guardian. But then when she dies Rose takes on the other girl's identity. However, in England Rose becomes a victim of her new guardian's greed and her life is threatened. Can she yet find love and happiness?

# SMILE OF A STRANGER

## Mavis Thomas

When Ruth Stafford joins her mother at the Sea Winds Hotel, she has misgivings about Cecily Stafford's imminent marriage to Willard Enderby. Ruth suspects he has designs on her mother's recent legacy. If so, she is determined to unmask him! She is helped by another hotel guest, and finds herself falling deeply in love with him . . . but is this endearing stranger any more trustworthy than Willard? Joys, heartbreaks and divided loyalties lie ahead before her questions find answers.

# CRANHAMS' CURIOS

## Chrissie Loveday

After her hectic London life, Rachel returns to her native Cornwall and her parents' Curio shop. Things are changing and she realises that she is needed. There is plenty to do and the local vet, Charlie is an added incentive to extend her stay . . . but he has a serious girlfriend. Can she make a new life in St Truan or will she miss the city life? Will she stay for just a week or is it a lifetime commitment?